Y0-DCF-441

# TAXI DRIVER

# &

# BALLERINA

*A NOVELLA*

*BY*

**KENNY LEE**

# COPYRIGHT

Taxi Driver & Ballerina

Copyright © 2025 Kenny Lee
All rights reserved. No portion of this book may be reproduced in any
form without permission from the publisher, except as permitted by
U.S. copyright law.

Print
ISBN: 978-1-959119-09-8

2nd Edition 2025

Published by
ImprintPublisher
Monterey, CA 93940

# CHAPTER 1

JOE SANDERS DROVE a taxi in San Francisco. He was rather proud of his job, even though it wasn't the so-called "respectable job" for a college graduate with a BA in philosophy. Aside from making a living, driving a cab gave him many opportunities to meet people from all walks of life, thus the perfect environment to study human behaviors first-hand.

Since he liked driving, he didn't mind the long hours. He just liked the idea of taking someone from point A to point B.

He stayed at a residence club, which provided room and board. There were recreational facilities like a pool and ping-pong tables. Sometimes, people got together and played poker. Joe was not a bad player, but lately, he'd had a streak of bad luck that resulted in three straight losses. Although it was not high stakes, like any other gambling, even a nickel ante and dime raise could amount to quite a bit of money over the long run. The losing streak made Joe worry about next month's rent, so he decided to pawn one of his most valuable possessions, a Nikon camera.

When he dropped an elderly woman off near the pawnshop he had frequented before, he parked his cab and went into the store with his camera. As he entered, he noticed the owner, Sam Giovani, behind the counter. He was a man with a receding hairline, protruding belly, and a round chubby face that looked even more round with his round-shaped spectacles. He looked suspiciously over his glasses at Joe.

"What can I do for you today?"

"I want to pawn this...How much can I get?"

The owner checked the camera by clicking the shutter and looking at the lens.

"You don't want to sell it?"

"No, I just want to pawn it."

"How much do you want?"

"500"

Sam tightened his lips, shook his head, and looked over the camera one more time to pick out any defects.

"I'll give you 400 max."

"This is a Nikon, and it's brand new!" Joe protested.

"I know, I know...but that's the best I can do for you if you just want to pawn it."

Sam shrugged and went over to the other customer

who had been waiting. Joe stood there staring at the seemingly infinite variety of items sprawled all over the storage cabinets and on its walls. He couldn't help wondering where all these items came from and what untold stories lay behind the people who had decided to pawn them. After a while, Sam came back to Joe.

"Well, have you decided what to do?"

"O.K., I'll settle for 400...I must say you're one tough businessman, Sam."

"Hey, don't blame me, Joe...the name of the game is making money... I want to be nice to everybody, but then I die starving."

After Joe signed the promissory note, Sam opened the cash register and put the money on the counter. Joe grabbed the money and put it in his pocket. As he was leaving, he turned around and said.

"Don't worry, Sam, nobody will ever accuse you of being too generous."

When Joe walked out of the pawnshop, his eyes met those of a prostitute. She looked in her mid-twenties, dressed provocatively; she had on a leotard with a low neckline showing her full bustline as well as tight jeans that showed off her well-proportioned body. When Joe was about to open the driver's side door of his cab, she asked.

"Are you working?"

"Yeah, where do you want to go?"

She got into the cab.

"Take me to the Sheraton...I heard a hundred Japanese businessmen just came for a conference."

"Sure."

On the way to the hotel, she started to put more make-up on her face.

"I've never seen you before. What's your name?"

"Joe." As he looked at her in the rearview mirror.

"What's yours?"

"April."

"How's business lately?"

"It's alright...I used to average a thousand, but lately only $800."

"Per week?"

"No, per day."

"That much?"

"That's nothing, honey!... If I really hustle, I can make a lot more."

She said rather nonchalantly.

"Maybe I'm in the wrong job...I bust my ass all day just to make a hundred bucks."

April started to giggle uncontrollably, but Joe couldn't figure out what he said was so amusing to her.

"Joe, if you were to do my kind of job, you'd bust your rear... I mean literally." and she giggled some more.

When he dropped her off at the Sheraton, many customers were waiting for cabs, but he waved them off since he didn't want to be late for the evening shift driver. Joe and the evening shift driver had gotten into an argument once, and he tried not to do it again.

Joe used to work the evening shift, but for some reason, he now preferred the day shift. While waiting for his cab to be gassed up and have a general engine check-up, which was required at the end of each shift at Yellow Cab Headquarters, Joe took out the money from his pocket to see how much he made. He must cover many charges like cab rental fees, gasoline fees, and tips to 'various headquarters workers like cab and radio dispatchers and maintenance mechanics. These tips were not mandatory, but those who didn't pay usually ended up with old and poor working-conditioned cabs most of the time.

Most new drivers quickly learned that paying the tips was much better than getting hassled all the time.

When Joe signed off and got into his car, it was 5 PM. Driving all day long was very tiring, but it also gave him a sense of natural high for knowing he did his job well to the best of his ability. The music on the radio and the soft breeze through the opened window caressed his face; everything pleased him. He thought even the people on the street waiting for the bus were waving at him.

Tomorrow may bring a new set of problems to tackle, but for now, his heart raced with joy when he thought about the rest of the evening consisting of having a relaxing dinner with fellow residents and, after that, possibly having another round of poker.

The Kenmore Residence Club Joe stayed in was a medium-sized hotel that had been converted into a boardinghouse. It had a big lobby with a huge mirror on the wall and a dining room that could easily accommodate about 50 people at one time. The TV room was next to the dining room. In the basement, there was a laundry room, ping-pong, and pool tables for its guests.

Aside from the benefit of providing room and board, the Residence Club's major selling point was its location: it was situated just eight blocks from downtown, and within a few blocks, there were many restaurants and bars as well as all kinds of stores. This was ideal for people who didn't have cars like most transients and for those who couldn't afford a car since they lived on fixed incomes.

The place was usually full, although the average stay of its guests was 2 weeks. The Club never seemed to have trouble attracting new tenants. It was a meeting place for people from all walks of life and many countries.

Casual talks between strangers in the lobby after dinner would very often turn into stimulating conversations about politics, philosophy, religion, and topics of all sorts. Some tenants who came down to buy a soft drink or to watch TV would be drawn into a discussion and ended up participating for hours.

To Joe, this kind of activity was the best part of living in the Club. Like all big cities, San Francisco can be a lonely place, and meeting people is not easy. However, the people who stayed felt like they were living in a commune. There were drawbacks to not having much privacy, not much choice of food they provided each day, or putting up with people one didn't get along with. However, for Joe, it was a fair tradeoff.

When Joe arrived at the Club, he went straight to the front desk and checked his mail slot to see if he had any mail, but it was empty. Then he went to the dining room, which was full of fellow boarders. He went to the salad bar first and looked around to decide where to sit. He saw a table with many of his poker buddies: Larry the lawyer, Jim the accountant, Dale the car salesman, and Eddy the piano player turned semi-professional card shark.

"Hi, guys," Joe said

"Sit down, Joe. How was your day?" asked Larry, his mouth full of spaghetti.

"It was hectic as always."

"Joe, we're gonna start early tonight," said Eddy.

"Is anyone else playing beside you guys?" said Joe.

"Two cabbies, they drive for Luxor. You'll just love the action they give you," said Eddy.

"I hate to say this, but compared to you, everybody plays loose," said Jim

Suddenly, Eddy's exuberant face turned gloomy.

"Jim, are you calling me a Rock?" Eddy snapped at Jim

"I am not calling you anything."

"Then shut up!" Eddy yelled.

"Oh, this is great!... Can we have dinner without arguing for Christ's sake?" Larry said as he put his fork down.

Everybody was quiet for a moment and just ate. When Joe turned his head to his right, he was surprised to see a young brunette whom he had never seen before having dinner alone at a corner table. He couldn't help but keep turning his head to look at her. She was young and beautiful, but that was not the primary reason why Joe felt such a strong attraction toward her. Her appearance and mannerisms exuded a kind of unique sophistication and class. Joe wanted to go over there and talk to her, but he couldn't think of any good opening line.

Talking had resumed at his table, but he couldn't hear anything except their moving mouths. Finally, Joe gathered up the courage to go over and talk to her. He was willing to accept any outcome: rejection, humiliation, or whatever. Although it was only a few steps from his table to hers, he thought they were the longest seven steps he had ever taken.

"Hi, you must be new."

She looked up and smiled, "Yes."

"Oh, allow me to introduce myself...My name is Joe. What's yours?"

"I'm Debbie."

"May I sit down?"

"Of course."

Joe sat down, but he didn't know what else to say. Just looking at the gorgeous woman in front of him made his heart pump rapidly. Instinctively, he knew he had to say something to get some sort of conversation going. With each passing second, it got more awkward.

"So, tell me, Debbie, what a nice girl like you doing in a place like this?"

Debbie smiled without responding right away.

"I thought you already had a good opening line."

"Oh, did I?...O.K. then let me change that to...where are you from?"

"From Melbourne."

"Australia?"

"Yes."

"That's a long way from here."

"I've always wanted to come to America but never had a chance to do so until now."

"That's great!... Would you mind if I showed you around the city?"

Debbie didn't know how to respond to this offer but managed to say, "Hmmm...sure."

Debbie looked at Joe, trying to figure out what kind of man he was. Joe felt her probing eyes.

"You don't sound too sure," Joe said.

"Well, I must say...you're a little too suave...My mother said to watch out for suave men."

"Trust me, Debbie. I'm totally harmless."

This remark made Debbie laugh.

"Harmless?... I don't know whether that's good or bad."

"It all depends on what you want, doesn't it? Joe smiled, and Debbie thought he had a nice smile. They both looked at each other for a moment.

"What kind of work do you do?" asked Debbie.

"Do you really want to know what I do for a living?"

"Yes."

"I'm a pimp."

Suddenly, Debbie's eyes were wide open and broke into laughter.

"You what?"

"No, I'm just kidding...but not too far off either...I drive a cab."

"Oh, why do you say that?"

"Well, for one thing, we both work the street."

She laughed again.

"You have a point there, Joe...It must be fun to meet all kinds of people."

"Yeah, I like it...but I also meet a lot of crazy people, too, and this city is full of them."

The dining room was almost empty. Larry, in his late fifties, who is tall and skinny, came by the table on his way out.

"Hey, young lady, watch out for this guy."

"Hi, Larry. This is Debbie," said Joe.

"Nice to meet you, Larry." She reached out for a handshake.

Larry stared at her while holding her hand and kissed it.

"What a beautiful girl you are, Debbie...If I were 10 years younger, I would've made a pass at you."

Debbie retracted her hand as she blushed.

"Get outta here, you dirty old man," said Joe, and Larry smiled mischievously.

"You gonna play tonight, Joe?"

"Maybe, but don't count me in."

Larry took another look at Debbie and said, "I don't blame you...see you later, folks!"

Joe and Debbie sat and talked until the dining staff began cleaning.

# CHAPTER 2

WHEN DEBBIE ENTERED HER ROOM, her roommate, Sherry Miller, was lying in bed reading a book. Like Debbie, she had come to San Francisco for a six-month ballet workshop, offered only to ballerinas with a reasonable prospect of becoming prima ballerinas in their respective troupes.

"Hi, Sherry."

"Hi, Debbie."

"Have you eaten yet?" asked Debbie.

"No, I just didn't feel like it. How was the food? Sherry said while looking at the book.

"Food was all right... I met a guy in the dining room... He's kind of nice."

Debbie went to the mirror stand to touch up her make-up. Sherry suddenly sat up on her bed and looked at Debbie.

"You did! What's his name?"

"Joe."

"What does he look like?"

"Well, he's kind of tall, but what's striking to me was he had such an intelligent and confident look about him... and I must say he's got a cute smile too."

"Sounds like you like him, Debbie."

Debbie stopped combing her hair and turned to Sherry.

"You think so? What makes you think that?"

"It's not so much what you said but how you said it."

"Oh, is it?... I can say he's witty and interesting, but I don't know about liking him. I just met him, Sherry."

Sherry looked at Debbie attentively as if probing some secret.

"So, did he ask you out?"

"Sort of... he said he wants to show me around the city."

"And what did you say?"

"I don't remember exactly what I said, but... I think I said yes."

"You think?... You don't remember?... Oh, my God!"

Sherry fell back onto the bed momentarily, then got up again.

"What does he do? Do you know?"

"He said he drives a cab."

"He's a cabbie?"

Sherry sounded surprised and disappointed at the same time.

"Yes, that's what he said," Debbie said casually, and when she turned her head to look at Sherry only to find her return to reading again.

Joe felt good about meeting Debbie, and he even felt like singing in the shower. When he came out of the shower, he saw his roommate, Barry Shaw, a free-lance sportswriter, reading a magazine and drinking beer.

"Hi, Barry."

"How's it going, Joe?... Who was the girl you talking to in the dining room?" he asked as he sipped the beer.

"Oh, did you see her?"

"Yeah, she's kinda cute... Where's she from?"

"She's from Australia," said Joe as he dried his hair with a towel.

"Australia?... Why did she come here?"

"I don't know... I didn't ask her, but I'm glad she came here, for whatever the reason is."

"I heard that some Australian chicks are pretty wild, and maybe she is fast and loose."

"Come on, Barry. No self-respecting women are fast and loose."

"Are you saying that you don't like women who play fast and loose?"

"No, you're missing my point... if a woman has any pride, she'll be choosy, that's all."

"Anyway, whatever you do, don't lose her because if you do, I'm gonna take my shot at her."

Barry's remarks sounded like a challenge, but Joe just smiled and walked away. After putting on new clothes, he went down to the lobby and picked up a newspaper to read. Soon, he heard people playing poker in the dining room. For some reason, he didn't feel his usual urge to play. He just sat there and read the newspaper for some time.

His thoughts wavered on whether to play poker or just go back to his room, but he finally decided to join the game. There were six players: Larry, Eddy, Dale, and Jim, and two cabbies: Fred and Sonny. Each player took a turn dealing, and the dealer chose the type of game that he wanted to play, like Texas Hold 'em, Low Ball, Five Card Stud, or Seven Card Stud.

"Let's play Seven Card Stud for a change," said Larry, blowing smoke from the corner of his mouth.

He wasn't a good player and lost money most of the time. However, when he didn't play cards, he went out to bars and got drunk. This often led him to be robbed or get into a fight. More than once, Joe had seen Larry being dumped from a cab in front of the residence club. His face would be bloody when it hit the pavement, and he couldn't get up because he was drunk. Joe and some other residents would have to pick him up and put him in bed.

The next morning in the dining room, old Larry

would be in a jovial mood, smiling as if nothing had happened yesterday even though he had some band-aid on his busted forehead. He had tried to quit drinking many times, and he finally succeeded, but after a year or two, he resumed. It wasn't because of a lack of will on his part; he concluded that life without drinking was just too boring and not worth living.

In his heyday, he had been one of the best criminal lawyers in the city and had made good money as well. He could afford to live in an expensive house and drive a luxury car, but three failed marriages and alcoholism had finally taken their toll on him. Even though he was only in his late fifties, his face and body easily looked ten years older. When he finished dealing, he shouted,

"I feel really lucky today... Let's build up the pot this time!"

"I will open it," Jim threw in 50 cents to the pot.

"I will call that and raise you." Dale threw in a dollar.

Eddy and Joe called the raise.

"Here is my one dollar, and I raise 50 more cents," said Sonny.

Fred examined his hand for a moment and called.

"So, since everybody is in, I will raise the pot without even looking at my hand," said Larry

By the time the last card was dealt, the pot had grown to almost $50. Everybody folded their hands except Joe and Larry were left to compete for the pot.

When Joe and Larry showed their hands, Joe had three Aces, but Larry made a straight, which was the winning hand for the pot.

"Sonofabitch!... I had three Aces from the start but just couldn't improve my hand," said Joe

"Joe, do you want to know why you lost that pot?" said Larry

"Look at this guy!... He just beat me out of a big pot, and now he wants to give me a lecture!" retorted Joe.

"Alright then, I won't tell you," Larry shrugged as he arranged the earnings from the last pot.

"Tell me, Larry, I want to hear it," Eddy insisted.

"As they say, if you're lucky with women, you're unlucky with cards and vice versa. Joe just met a girl, so I knew he wouldn't be lucky... It's an Old Wives' Tale, but somehow it's true."

"By the way, haven't you been married three times already, Larry?" Jim asked as he dealt.

"That's right."

"That shows how lousy you were in bed," said Jim.

Everybody laughed at the remark.

# CHAPTER 3

A FEW DAYS LATER, a charity ballet performance was given at the San Francisco Ballet Theater. Many people came to see the performance, all dressed in formal evening attire. Debbie and Sherry were scheduled to be in supporting roles, however, something unexpected forced Debbie to perform the lead role.

Her performance exceeded everyone's expectations. It received rave reviews from San Francisco Newspapers. The critics talked about what a talent she had and wondered why she wasn't a permanent member of the San Francisco Ballet Troupe and so on. Debbie was excited to receive so many compliments, and she called her parents to tell them the news.

As far as Debbie was concerned, this event helped her make up her mind as to what she wanted to do in her life: to become a prima ballerina. Even before coming to

America, she had been unsure of what she wanted to do with her life. She wasn't certain whether she had what it took to be a prima ballerina.

This also made her rethink her scheduled marriage to her fiancé, Arnold, in Australia. What was most important at this time of her life was fulfilling her lifelong dream of becoming an internationally recognized ballerina. She knew there would be stiff resistance from her parents and Arnold if she suggested any changes to their marriage plan. However, she was determined to live her life the way she wanted to.

The evening after her performance found Debbie at the residence club. Sherry was fixing her hair in front of the mirror as Debbie wrote a letter at her desk:

"Dear Arnold,

San Francisco is a wonderful place. I'm having a great time, but I also miss you very much. The workshop was not easy, but I didn't expect it to be, and I am learning a lot. I've made a lot of friends from many countries. My roommate, Sherry, is from Indiana..."

"Whom are you writing to?" asked Sherry

"My fiancé."

"I didn't know you were engaged."

"We had planned to get married last February, but I postponed it at the last minute."

"Why?"

"I've always wanted to come here. I thought it would be nice to travel alone before I got married."

"Do you love him?"

"Love?... I guess so... he's the only man I've been intimate with... but I still don't know what love means... I mean to love someone more than yourself."

"Do you think such love exists?"

"Wouldn't we all like to believe it exists?"

"Debbie, we women are such tragic creatures; we're slaves to love all our lives."

"Tragic? Why do you say tragic?... No one forces us to be that way."

Sherry couldn't respond to Debbie right away, instead, she just looked at the mirror and made a face of displeasure.

In the meantime, Joe sat by the phone and wondered whether to call Debbie or not. If she answered, what would he say? Many things went through his mind. He wondered whether she still remembered him or even his name. He finally picked up the phone.

"Hello, front desk? Room 306, please."

After a few ringing tones, Debbie picked up the phone.

"Hello."

"Hi, Debbie. How are you doing?"

"Oh, hi, Joe... how are you? I thought you'd never call."

She recognized his voice without him mentioning his name, this made him happy.

"I've been thinking about you all the time... It's just that I've been waiting for the right time to call you... you know the expression... timing is everything!"

This made her laugh heartily.

"How do you like it here so far?"

"It's just great. Everything is wonderful!"

"Glad to hear that... Are you still interested in me showing you around the city?"

There were a couple of seconds of silence.

"Well... I guess..." Her voice sounded a little tentative.

"Well, I guess?" Joe repeated. "That doesn't sound like a definite answer to me, Debbie."

Now, she had to say either yes or no. If she said no, he might never ask her again, and that crossed her mind. Besides, she liked how he made her laugh.

"Yes, I'm interested."

"OK, then, tomorrow is Saturday... Is tomorrow morning alright with you?"

"Yes, what time?"

"I'll see you at ten in the lobby."

"That's fine."

"See you tomorrow, Debbie."

"OK, see you, Joe."

When Joe hung up the phone, he let out a yell of triumph. At that very moment, Barry walked into the room.

"Must be some good news."

"I'm going out with Debbie."

"So, you're finally gonna check her out?"

"I'm just gonna show her around the city."

"Hey, hey, hey... who's better suited than you... the taxi driver himself."

"Stop teasing me, Barry... I don't intend to be a cabbie for life."

Why?. It's a perfectly honorable occupation, Joe."

"Well, it's a job, but not something that you brag about to your mother-in-law."

"Joe, trust me, any job is a good job if it pays your rent," said Barry as he started taking his clothes off to take a shower.

"I like my job, but it does have a price to pay."

"What's that?"

"It burns me out emotionally... I deal with so many people every day, it can drive you crazy sometimes."

"Well, nobody said making a living in a big city was easy, Joe."

Barry went into the shower and soon started singing.

# CHAPTER 4

Joe got up early the next morning. He took the time to pick the right clothes for the occasion. He decided to wear slacks and an Air Force leather bomber jacket. He waited for about twenty minutes for Debbie to come down. At five minutes past ten, she came down into the lobby wearing a red sweater and a pair of blue jeans; she had a small bag over her shoulder. Maybe it was her athletic figure; she had a look of perfect health and beauty.

"Hi," Joe greeted.

"Hi," Debbie responded.

"Are you ready?"

"Yes," Debbie said enthusiastically, and Joe motioned toward the door.

"Shall we?"

The two walked out the door towards Joe's orange

color VW convertible that was parked right in front of the residence club. The weather was sunny, although the wind was a little bit chilly.

They first went to the Marina district and saw a majestic view of the Golden Gate Bridge. Joe explained its history to Debbie: how they built it, what manpower was needed, how many people had died to accomplish this feat, what engineering miracles it took, and so on.

Then Joe drove over the bridge to Sausalito, where numerous neat shops and restaurants sprawled along the waters: many of the rich had built their houses on the hills overlooking San Francisco Bay. The city's skyline appeared like a mystical city rising above the ocean on a foggy day.

He took her to a restaurant called Spinnaker, where two-thirds of the building was on the water, which gave one the illusion of dining on a boat. It had one of the best angles to view San Francisco stretching out across the bay. Even Debbie, who had seen many beautiful places in Melbourne and Sydney, couldn't help but be impressed with the view. Joe knew this restaurant well since he had worked as a busboy when he first came to San Francisco.

After lunch, they went back to the city and visited Fisherman's Wharf and Chinatown; Debbie did some shopping for souvenirs as well. Then Joe thought it would be nice to take her to Twin Peaks for panoramic views of the entire city and the bay. When they reached the mountain top, the wind was rather strong, however, the clear weather allowed them to see for miles and miles in all directions.

"Oh, my!... What a breathtaking view this is!" said Debbie.

She took a small pocket camera out of her bag and took pictures of the scenery and Joe. He, in turn, took her picture against the backdrop of the city. Joe even asked one of the other sightseers to take a picture of them, and he gladly obliged. After taking pictures, Joe started to explain what they were seeing.

"Is that the Golden Gate Bridge? Asked Debbie.

"No, the Golden Gate Bridge is over there." he turned around and pointed to it.

"That's the Bay Bridge," Joe said to Debbie, whose long brunette hair was flying in the brisk wind.

"I see... What's across the bridge?"

"The city of Oakland."

"I see... Where's Berkeley?"

"That's a little bit to the left of Oakland."

"I've heard a lot about that school."

"Do you want to go over there?"

"Sure... but do you have time?"

"Did you ask me whether I have time?... Let's put it this way... I have nothing but time, Debbie."

Joe's theatrical gestures and remarks made Debbie laugh.

"Let's go then," said Debbie.

It was a wonderful drive to Berkeley over the Bay Bridge they had just seen from the Twin Peaks. The soft music on the radio, the wind, and the nice warm touch of sunlight were most idyllic. When Debbie closed her eyes to savor the moment, something suddenly reminded her of the movie scene from The Graduate, where the main protagonist, Dustin Hoffman, and his girlfriend, played by Katherine Ross, were passing over this very bridge in his open convertible Alfa Romeo.

"Have you seen the movie The Graduate?" asked Debbie.

"Yes, a long time ago when I was in High school."

"Crossing this bridge in this convertible reminds me of it."

"Did you like the movie?" asked Joe.

"I thought it was romantic."

"I remember it vaguely; I didn't know what the main issue was in the movie... All I remember is the theme songs by Simon and Garfunkel... other than that, I didn't think it was anything memorable," said Joe, shrugging his shoulders.

"Oh, another thing about that movie was... Katherine Ross reminded me of a girl I used to know."

"Was she your first love?"

"Come to think of it... yeah, she was... How did you guess?"

"Let's just say it's a woman's intuition."

. . .

They arrived at the Berkeley campus around 3 PM. They walked around the campus and talked about all the student demonstrations during the Vietnam War era. Their walk eventually led to Telegraph Hill Street, where many restaurants, coffee shops, and bookstores catered to the students and visitors.

All the walking made their feet tired, so they went into one of the coffee shops; the place was crowded with students: the music coming out of the speakers was Jazz. They sat at a table and ordered two Cappuccinos. Debbie looked around and saw lots of students; some were discussing something in a heated manner, and some just closed their eyes, either meditating or just listening to the music. They seemed full of idealism, unworried about the harsh reality of making a living.

The slow-turning ceiling fans with their large blades, colorful forest decorations on the walls, and the music created an atmosphere like she was in an exotic place.

"Did you go to school here?" asked Debbie, sipping Cappuccino.

"No, I went to a small private University."

"What did you study?"

"A lot of useless stuff."

"Useless stuff?... Why is that?"

"I don't know... I just never liked school."

"What was your major?"

"Philosophy."

"Philosophy?... sounds interesting though."

"Yeah, I guess... but try to get a job with a BA in Philosophy... it's tough luck."

Debbie pondered for a moment and asked.

"But since you earned a degree in it, you must have liked it, Joe."

"Yes, I did... I love philosophy!"

"Since I don't know anything, can you tell me something about it?"

Joe paused for a moment before he spoke. Debbie liked the way he pondered things before he spoke.

"It's the study of fundamental nature of knowledge, reality, and existence... but it's about us, about the man."

Debbie nodded without fully understanding the meaning of it, but she liked the sound of it.

"I still remember the first day of my philosophy class. The professor gave us homework to write about the definition of man... we were all puzzled. I thought about it all day and finally came up with something to write about."

"What was that?" asked Debbie inquisitively, putting her face closer to Joe.

"I wrote that man is an animal who was able to develop a spoken as well as written language... from which he became aware of morality since language itself contains morality like good and evil, love and hate, construction and destruction, and so on. From this moral awareness, man invented god and religion... This is the fundamental difference between man and other animals, that they do not have a god or religion, since they don't have a sense of morality, which as I said comes from languages, especially written ones."

"Wow... that's a very interesting idea. So, is it safe to assume that you don't believe in God?"

"Maybe not in the traditional sense, but I firmly believe in the value of religion to mankind. Just look at all the man-made structures like pyramids and fantastic churches and temples around the world since the dawn of human civilization. Man built it for honoring gods."

"Do you go to church?" asked Debbie.

"I still go to church now and then, but I think ultimately man created god, not the other way around."

Debbie laughed at the remark. It sounded so ludicrous and yet logical according to his definition of man. She was impressed with his ability to analyze such a profound philosophical question. Although she had never had this kind of discussion with anyone in her life, she was enjoying the conversation. She started to think of him as someone unique.

"That is a very ironic stateman, Joe."

"Yes, I know... but life is full of ironies, isn't it? Joe shrugged.

"What did the professor say about your paper?"

"He said that he had never heard or read anything like what I wrote, but it sounded to him like a very logical definition of man. He also said I am one of those rare original thinkers. To me, that was the highest compliment that I ever received, and he urged me to keep thinking."

"Have you been doing that? Thinking."

"Yes, I'm always thinking... I couldn't stop it even if I wanted to."

"About what?"

"About everything under the sun!... Enough about me, Debbie. Let's talk about you."

"I'm afraid my life story is boring, and there's not much to tell you."

"Let me be the judge of that."

"OK, then ask me... What do you want to know?' said Debbie as she touched her hair and playfully looked at him.

"Everything."

"Everything?"

"Yes, I want to know everything about you."

Joe rested his chin in his cupped hands and looked at her admiringly. However, she just threw her head back and laughed.

"How can I tell you everything when I don't even know everything myself?"

"That's very true... but I think you know what I mean."

She tried to compose herself.

"Alright, seriously, what do you want to know about me?"

Joe smiled mischievously but soon put on a serious face and spoke.

"How about you start with your measurements?"

Incredulous to what she had just heard, her eyes opened wide. A moment later, she grabbed a teaspoon from the table and threw it at Joe. The spoon barely missed Joe as he dodged.

They left Berkeley at dusk. As they drove back to San Francisco over the Bay Bridge, the sun was setting against the backdrop of the city skyline, a view often seen in city postcards. Joe and Debbie felt they knew each other so much more than when they drove over this bridge the other way. Joe thought about the old cliché "What a difference a day makes." but in this case, "a few hours."

When they arrived in the city, the logical thing to do was to go back to the residence club and have dinner since it was still dinner hour, but neither of them wanted to do that. They didn't want their date to end so soon, even though they had spent practically a whole day together; somehow, time flew by for them.

The other reason was among the many benefits the club offered to its guests; food was not one of its strong areas. At times, some guests would complain openly to the management, only to receive a response like "We're doing the best we can with a limited budget." However, what they want to say is, "What do you expect from the money you're paying?"

"I know this nice restaurant, and the food was great last time I ate there," said Joe, and he looked at Debbie for a response.

"I have no objection to that."

The restaurant was situated on the edge of a cliff overlooking the Pacific Ocean, so the restaurant was named Cliff-House. When they entered, the place was full, and there was a long waiting list. Joe slipped a twenty-dollar bill to the head waiter as he jotted Joe's name on the list. After a short wait, Joe's name was called on by the speaker.

They were seated at a window table, where they could see the ocean at night with the help of spotlights situated on the roof of the restaurant. The ocean at night seemed to have a mysterious and fearsome beauty. From the table, they could see and feel the huge waves hitting the cliff walls rhythmically, with tremendous power.

"Joe, you really know how to give a city tour, I must say," as she sipped her cocktail, Margarita.

"Did you enjoy it?"

"Oh, yes, absolutely!... I had the time of my life."

"I'm glad you did."

"What a wonderful place this is... I don't think I'll ever get tired of living here!"

"It's funny you said that. That's what I thought when I got here."

"You don't feel like that, now?"

"Well, when you drive a cab like me, you see everything... beauty as well as ugliness," Joe said pensively.

"Ugliness? Such as?"

"Crimes, Homeless people, Drug Addicts, and Prostitution...you name it, they have it right here."

"It's very sad, isn't it?"

"Yes, it is... I see these every day, and yet the city has such a beautiful façade. I started to think this beautiful exterior was a mask to cover the true face of its ugliness. And that's when I realized that I don't like living here all that much!"

Debbie glanced at Joe, whose eyes had no focus but a blank stare outside.

"That's an interesting way to describe the city."

"I believe there are two kinds of beauty... warm beauty and cold beauty. This city definitely has the cold one."

Debbie thought about it for a moment and asked.

"Then what is your definition of warm beauty?"

"I knew you were going to ask me that... When something is real, not fake, it produces a certain warmth from within. The beauty that invokes a certain feeling...like you."

Debbie blushed a little and said, "Thank you."

"Here is to you, Debbie," the two toasted their drinks and looked out the window.

Finally, the waiter brought their food. It was a long wait, but, on this occasion, they didn't mind it at all.

When they arrived at the club, it was a little past nine. There was no one in the lobby. As they waited for the elevator, Joe saw the desk clerk waving hello from behind the window. The old elevator came down with a big thumping sound. There were no other people besides Joe and Debbie. As the elevator went up, Joe looked at Debbie, and in their gaze, they felt a strong attraction. Joe touched her hand, and when he tried to kiss her, the elevator stopped and its door wide open.

An elderly lady with a cane looked bewildered when she saw young people in an embrace. Joe and Debbie got off with sheepish grins.

Joe walked Debbie to her room, and before he did anything, Debbie blocked his lips with her index finger.

"Good night, Joe. I had a wonderful time."

"Good night, Debbie."

She opened the door and went in. The moment Sherry saw Debbie, she knew it was a good date.

"It must have been a good one, Debbie."

Debbie just nodded and took her shoes off, then threw herself onto her bed.

"Where did you go?" asked Sherry curiously.

"We went to so many places, and I had a wonderful time. The date was so much better than I expected...He is so..."

"He's so what, Debbie?"

When she didn't hear Debbie's response, she went over. Debbie already closed her eyes and seemed to have fallen asleep, hugging her pillow.

When Sherry looked at Debbie, it was a picture of contentment, and she could only imagine what made it so.

# CHAPTER 5

DEBBIE'S FATHER, William Mulligan, was a proud man who firmly believed in family and work ethic. He was a good businessman as well. He made millions through an electronics company called New Age Electronics, a company he had founded with his high school buddy, Albert McMurry, right after college.

The company now employed fifteen thousand workers and was the third largest company in Melbourne. Mr. McMurry was CEO and Chairman of the board, and Mr. Mulligan was President. Mr. Mulligan lived in an affluent neighborhood in a big mansion surrounded by manicured lawns and tall trees. The family had had a houseman, Fred Jackson, a Jamaican native, for the last fifteen years.

A Jaguar sports car pulled up in front of Mr. Mulligan's house entrance. Out came a tall, blond, well-built man wearing sunglasses who looked like a movie star. His name was Arnold McMurry, the only son of Albert McMurry. He had been carefully groomed since his college graduation to succeed his father and currently held the position of executive vice-president of the marketing division.

When Fred opened the door and saw him, he was most courteous since he knew how important a guest Arnold was to the Mulligan family.

"Well, good morning, Mr. McMurry. Come on in, sir," said Fred as he bowed gently.

"Hi Fred, is Mr. Mulligan in?"

"Yes, sir... I'll call him right away. Won't you have a seat?" and Fred scurried away.

The house's interior was decorated with many European antiques and Dutch paintings from the 17th and 18th centuries. While Arnold was waiting, he looked at family pictures on the wall. In one picture, Debbie and her family are shown celebrating her high school graduation. In another shot, Debbie was performing in front of a large crowd. Soon, Mr. and Mrs. Mulligan showed up to greet Arnold.

"Hi, Arnold. How are you? What a pleasant surprise, you drop in on us like this!" said Mrs. Mulligan as she hugged him, hardly containing her joy.

"Hello, Mrs. Mulligan... I was just passing by, so I thought I'd just say hello to you."

"Oh, that's so sweet of you, Arnold."

"You look good. How's everything?" said Mr. Mulligan as he shook hands.

"Things are going well, sir."

Afterward, they all went into the living room.

"Please do sit down, Arnold," said Mrs. Mulligan.

When he did so, Mrs. Mulligan motioned toward Fred, who was standing in the corner.

"Fred, why don't you bring us some tea?"

"Certainly, Madam."

"How is Mrs. McMurry?" asked Mrs. Mulligan.

"She always manages to keep herself busy with all kinds of activities," said Arnold.

"Oh, yes, what a marvelous woman she is."

"I sure hope I'm still that active at her age," said Arnold, and Debbie's parents laughed.

There was silence for a moment, but it was broken when Fred brought tea.

"Arnold, you're staying for dinner, aren't you? said Mrs. Mulligan after sipping her tea.

"I have some meetings to attend this afternoon."

"Please, Arnold... you're going to break my heart if you don't."

She pleaded her case, holding his hand firmly.

"In that case, I guess everything just has to wait," said Arnold with a smile.

"That is so sweet of you... I'll leave you two men alone now."

She went over to Fred.

"I'd like a seafood dish and the best Chardonnay in the cellar for dinner," she said in a hushed voice.

Mr. and Mrs. Mulligan genuinely liked Arnold and thought he would be perfect for Debbie. Since they didn't have a son, they already thought of him as their own. They liked everything about him: good manners, a tall physique as well as a handsome face, and a bright future of running a successful company. They couldn't think of anything they didn't like about him.

"How is your work?" asked Mr. Mulligan

"The job is challenging, but it's a critical part of our company's success. So, I'm committed to doing it well," said Arnold with confidence.

"I see that you have your father's business acumen. You know, your father and I were voted in high school as the ones most likely to succeed."

"I've heard that those predictions are usually wrong, but I guess this time they were right on the money, Mr. Mulligan."

The two men shared a laugh, but soon after, a long silence ensued.

"Arnold, I know you came here for a reason... What is it, son?"

"Oh, it's nothing important... but have you heard from Debbie lately?"

"I think she called last Thursday and said she was having a wonderful time there... Why, Arnold, hasn't she called you?"

"We used to talk... but now she seems to prefer letters," said Arnold with a worried look.

"Why don't you call yourself rather than waiting for her?"

"I tried a few times already, but with the time difference and her schedule and everything, it's not easy catching her."

"Don't you worry, my boy... She'll be here in just four more months. I'm sure she is dying to see you!"

As Arnold listened, he just nodded.

# CHAPTER 6

BACK IN THE RESIDENCE CLUB, Joe, Debbie, Sherry, and Barry went downstairs after dinner to play pool. As they were playing, Barry asked Debbie.

"Have you ever been to a baseball game?"

"No, I haven't... Is that something like "Cricket?"... We play that game back in Australia," said Debbie.

"I don't know about Cricket, but if you haven't seen a baseball game, I think you ought to... It's a great American game."

"Oh, I'd love to."

"Great, I just happen to have four tickets for this Saturday's game. How about we all go there?"

He looked at Sherry and Joe.

"Fine with me," said Sherry.

"Who's playing?" asked Joe.

"It's the Giants versus the Dodgers... now, Joe, you can't miss that!"

"This Saturday, I'm scheduled to work, but I can get a replacement."

"Fantastic! We can all go in my car," Barry said.

"Are they good teams?" Debbie asked.

"This year they aren't so hot, but it doesn't matter... whenever they play each other it's very competitive because of the traditional rivalry between them."

Barry seemed more than happy to explain baseball history to two ballerinas who couldn't care about the two teams' rivalry. However, out of courtesy, the two girls paid attention to him as he elaborated.

The day they went to watch the baseball game was a gorgeous sunny day. Many people came out to see the game. Among the huge crowd were Barry, Sherry, Debbie, and Joe, eating peanuts and nachos while watching the game. The crowd roared whenever a Giants team member made a hit or made a catch.

"Why is he safe on first base?" Debbie asked Joe.

"Because he got there before the ball."

"I see... now what is he trying to do?"

"He's trying to steal second base."

"How does he do that?"

"Well... just watch that guy."

The man on the first base attempted to steal the second base, but he was thrown out by the catcher. There was a huge roar.

"Debbie, the ball got to the second baseman, and he tagged him before the player stole the base, and that's why the umpire called him out," Joe explained, using hand gestures.

"I guess it's going to take a while for me to understand this game."

The beer vendor went by, calling out, "beer here." "Hey beer," Joe called him back.

"How many?"

"Four."

While Joe was paying for the beer, a Giants hit a home run. When the crowd rose to their feet, the guy's head, who was in front of Joe, knocked beer over as he got up. The beer spilled all over, some on the man's face, some on Joe's clothes, and some on Debbie. They all laughed hilariously. The unexpected mishap was the highlight of their outing. Although the Giants eventually lost, the game was exciting up to the ninth inning.

# CHAPTER 7

ALBERT MCMURRY WAS a shy and private man by nature. He avoided socializing with others, except for the Mulligan family. However, for some reason, he decided to have a huge party for his 60th birthday. He even hired a professional band to make it more grandiose. He invited everybody that he knew. All who were invited felt extremely honored, knowing this was a once-in-a-lifetime occasion. Of course, Mr. and Mrs. Mulligan were the first to receive an invitation.

Among the guests were many rich and famous people. On the day of the party, waiters and waitresses walked around with trays of champagne glasses and caviar for the honored guests as the band played the music.

"Hello, Nancy, Bill...I'm glad you could come,"

said Mr. McMurry as he shook hands with Mr. Mulligan and kissed both cheeks of Mrs. Mulligan.

"Why, Al, I wouldn't miss this party for the world," Debbie's father said.

"It's so good to see you…what a lovely party this is," Mrs. Mulligan said with a polite smile.

"It must've cost you a bundle, Al," said Mr. Mulligan. Mr. McMurry laughed heartily.

"Well, as you can see, I'm not going to be young forever…all these years of working, I've never had much time to enjoy myself…What's the use of making a lot of money…I'm certainly not going to take it with me to the grave."

Everybody laughed. At that moment, Mrs. McMurry came over.

"Well, hello…Nancy, Bill…How are you?"

"I'm just delighted, thank you." Mrs. Mulligan said.

"Arnold told me that he stopped by your house a week ago."

"Oh, I enjoyed his company so much. What a nice, handsome young man he is…I'm so proud that he's going to be my son-in-law."

"Oh, Nancy, you're always so kind…" They took drinks from a waitress and made a toast.

"Joan, maybe we should set a tentative wedding date since Debbie is going to return in September," Mrs. Mulligan said.

"Why, that's a wonderful idea, Nancy," and they made a toast again as they laughed.

The band started to play up-tempo music, and a singer started to sing. The party was in full swing, as everybody seemed to be enjoying themselves, dancing, drinking, and talking. There were about seven hundred people, among them politicians, movie stars, well-known fashion designers, novelists, powerful business-men, and so on. The guest list read very much like the Who's Who of Australia's rich and famous.

The party took place in the back of Mr. McMurry's mansion, which had a huge lawn and patios decorated with exotic flowers and water fountains and from which the fabulous natural beauty of the forest and ocean were visible.

Later, Mr. and Mrs. McMurry went up to the stage to thank the guests.

"My distinguished guests, I am deeply honored that so many of you could come to help celebrate my 60th birthday…The reason that I decided to have my birthday in this grand fashion is that I suddenly realized I may not have many more of these birthdays…" The people laughed and applauded.

"Today, I would like to introduce to you my very special and dear friends of forty-five years, soon to be my in-laws…Mr. and Mrs. Mulligan," he motioned them to come up to the stage, and they obliged. When they got up and stood next to the McMurrays and waved their hands, the people applauded loudly. The band started to play a waltz, and the two couples started to dance.

# CHAPTER 8

On Sundays in Golden Gate Park, many rules and activities were different from other days. No cars were allowed inside the park, so people on bikes or roller skates could freely roam without the fear of being hit. Free live orchestra music was conducted in the open-air music hall, which was situated in the center between the De Young Museum and the Science Museum, the two most popular places in the park. There were many rows of wooden benches in front of the stage, which could accommodate several hundred people, but most young people preferred to sit on the green, which was located on either side of the benches. Many young sun worshippers enjoyed sunbathing while listening to the music, as professional orchestras played some of the finest classical pieces.

One Sunday, Debbie and Joe were among the crowd

on the grass appreciating the classical music, the sunshine, and each other's company. Debbie, a ballerina, was no stranger to this kind of music. She had also begun playing violin when she was only seven years old. She loved it so much that at one point in her life, she almost chose music over ballet.

"Do you like classical music?" asked Joe.

"Yes, I do…very much," she said as she turned her head and smiled.

"Who is your favorite?"

"I like Mozart, but Beethoven is my favorite."

"Is that right? What about his music appeals to you?" asked Joe. She thought about it for a moment.

"It's very intense and serious."

"Something intense and serious appeals to you?"

"Yes, it does…I've always liked passionate things." Debbie lay down with her hands under her head and looked at the blue sky. Joe turned his head and looked at her momentarily before lying down beside her. There was a moment of silence.

"Why did you ask that question?" asked Debbie.

"About the composer or your personality?"

"About the composer."

Without responding to her, he turned sideways to look at her. Her round forehead, prominent nose, and full lips were those of a classical beauty; her profile reminded him of a movie actress, Deborah Kerr. He picked a blade of grass and ran it from the bridge of her nose to her lips as he said, "I heard once from a man who claimed to study women all of his life that to know the true class of a woman, one has to ask about her preference in classical music and the one who picks Beethoven has class…real class."

"Why is that?"

"According to him, women with class almost always possess the qualities of seriousness and certain passion that correspond with the characteristics of Beethoven's music."

"Hmmm…Are you sure someone told you that…I have to think about that." As Joe played with the blade of grass on her face, neck, and ear, she felt an extremely ticklish sensation but was determined not to rub it away with her hand. The more she endured, the more she felt a certain sexual arousal. Joe felt that in her breathing and quivering lips.

"Joe, do you think I have class?" She looked at Joe with yearning eyes and lips slightly parted.

"Yes, I do…more than any woman I've ever met." Their eyes were fixed on each other. Joe lowered his head to meet hers, and when their lips finally met, it was a passionate kiss. Just then, the music ended, and the conductor turned around to accept loud applause from the audience. But to Joe and Debbie, in their euphoric state of union, it seemed as though the crowd was applauding their kiss.

There comes a time when spoken words are no

longer necessary between two people. Joe and Debbie felt like that after this passionate kiss.

Without a word, they knew exactly what they wanted, and nothing was going to stop them. The sexual attraction that Debbie and Joe felt was so strong that it overcame all their rationality and inhibitions. The urge to mate is one of the strongest desires. It is similar to what solitary animals like tigers feel during the mating season.

They went to a motel alongside Ocean Boulevard at the end of Golden Gate Park and made a long and passionate love. Afterward, the two lay still, exhausted, hands intertwined.

"How was it, Joe?" she said in a hushed voice.

"It was beautiful."

"I didn't know sex could be this wonderful..."

"You mean...this is..."

"Yes...quite unbelievable, isn't it?"

"No, I wouldn't say that..." They were silent for a while.

"I just wanted to experience it before I get married."

"Before you get married?"

"Yes, because I want to be a faithful wife once I get married." Joe felt a little hurt at her last remark, and he let go of her hand.

"So, you're doing it like...a kind of experiment?"

"Well...I guess you could say that...or at least that's what I thought...but I'm afraid that I am beginning to like you…a lot." She turned and lay on her stomach.

"You have a boyfriend back home?" Debbie just nodded and said, "We're planning to get married when I return."

"Do you want to?" Joe asked her in earnest. Debbie turned around to grab a sheet and covered her face.

"I don't know, Joe…I just don't know what I want anymore…" She seemed to be crying underneath the sheet. He felt bad that she was in turmoil and that he might be the cause of it. Joe uncovered her face.

"Don't worry, Debbie…I'll make sure you know what you want." He hugged her gently and kissed her teary eyes and lips lightly, but their kisses soon turned passionate once again.

# CHAPTER 9

DEBBIE AND SHERRY studied under the supervision of a Russian ballerina, Katerina Stoiyevna, who had once been a renowned prima ballerina in the famed Bolshoi ballet troupe for ten years before she had defected to America. She was in her sixties but was still in great physical shape and possessed considerable strength. She was very demanding of her students and never tolerated any excuses from them, accepting no less than 100%, even in practice sessions.

Although many young ballerinas wanted to learn from her, some did not appreciate her draconian style. She showed no mercy to those students who had no potential of becoming prima ballerinas. Not because she was a cold person by nature, but because she would rather have the students face the cruel reality and the truth of not having what it took to be a prima ballerina.

In fact, in her private life, she had shown generosity on more than a few occasions, such as donating money to homeless foundations or adopting a stray dog that she found in her neighborhood. However, as far as ballet was concerned, she was strict and merciless, as one must be in the pursuit of perfection.

A couple of days after their consummation, Joe dropped off a customer and realized how close he was to the ballet school that Debbie was attending.

Joe parked his cab and went into the building. When he entered, he could hear the music and the instructions of the teacher. He sat on a chair in the back row and observed the beauty and grace of the ballerinas' movements. Debbie moved like a butterfly on her toes. Her jumps and walking on her toes seemed to defy gravity.

He could hardly believe that just a couple of days ago, he had held her in his arms and made passionate love to her. She looked quite different on stage than the person he knew. Katerina's voice was like that of a Marine drill instructor. She made her students do the same movements over again and again until she was satisfied. Soon, the session ended with a lunch break. When Debbie spotted Joe, she waved her hand and came running to him. He could see the perspiration on her face. They exchanged a light kiss.

"Hi, aren't you supposed to be working?" said Debbie, wiping her forehead with a towel.

"Hey, I'm my own boss…I can take a break anytime I want to."

"Oh, that's nice…well, I'm glad you came…"

"Let's have lunch."

"O.K, but I'm on a diet…I really can't eat much."

"Come on, Debbie, right now, you're already as skinny as a chopstick. Why do you have to be thinner?" Although Joe said this half-jokingly, she took it personally.

"Joe, my profession requires me to watch what I eat, and besides, I don't look like a chopstick!" She snapped at Joe. He realized instantly he shouldn't have said it.

"O.K, O.K…I'm sorry, Debbie…I didn't mean to say it like that."

Debbie grudgingly accepted his apology and started to leave the building. Joe followed her.

They went to an Italian restaurant located only two blocks from the school. The place was crowded with regular lunch patrons, but they managed to get a table right away. A waiter took their orders and came back soon with their food and beverages.

"You looked pretty good when you were up on the stage," Joe said as he carefully examined her face to see whether she was still upset.

"Oh, you mean that?" her face lit up.

"Yeah, you kind of stood out…"

"Well, maybe because you know me…you know…

like a mother can always spot her child among the crowd."

"Maybe…at any rate, I thought you had a presence on the stage."

"Thank you, Joe…I'm very flattered…Now, this isn't your ploy to make up for what you said about me looking like a chopstick, is it?" Debbie looked at Joe suspiciously as if to see whether her assumption was correct.

"Come on, Debbie…What are you talking about? I would never lie to you about a thing like this…trust me," and he raised both arms.

"OK, Joe, but you kind of hurt my feelings when you said that."

"It was a joke, Debbie…Can't you take a joke?"

"I can take a joke…but not when it's about my figure…You have to understand that women are very self-conscious about these things."

Joe just rolled his eyes and said, "Oh, yes, I know!"

The waiter came over, took the finished plates, and said,

"Would you care for some dessert today?"

"No, I'll just have a cup of coffee," Joe said.

"And you, Miss?"

"Coffee, please."

As they drank coffee, Debbie broke the silence.

"Thank you, Joe."

"For what?"

"For coming to see me…" she said with a smile.

"Oh, not at all…I…I just had to see you, for some reason," and he scratched his forehead.

"Really?"

"Yes, I've been thinking about you all day," said Joe.

"That sounds sweet but also dangerous." "Dangerous? Why?" he said inquisitively. She smiled mischievously and said, "For one thing, since you're driving, you should be paying attention to the road."

Joe burst into laughter. "Why…you think I'm like some clumsy guy who can't walk and chew gum at the same time? OK, but if you think it's dangerous, then I won't do it, Debbie."

"I didn't tell you to stop it all together…I just said you should be careful, you dumbhead," and she gave him a mocked angry look.

"But seriously, Debbie, one can't shut one's thoughts on and off like a light switch…it just happens."

"I know what you mean…actually, I've been thinking about you, too," Debbie said shyly.

"Maybe it was telepathy…because I swear, something was telling me that I had to see you." He took her hand and kissed it.

"That sounds very romantic."

"Romantic? Yeah, I guess…but in some way, isn't it frightening that we don't have any control over our thoughts? Even what we like or dislike seems already programmed in us."

"If we don't have control over them, who do you think does?" she said with a curious look.

"Almighty God, of course...who else?" She looked a little puzzled at his rather nonchalant answer.

"But I thought that you didn't believe in God, Joe."

"Not necessarily God in a conventional sense, but I do firmly believe there is something that controls the universe...something that controls the harmony and balance."

"Joe, I must say you are something...When do you have the time to think about all this?"

"When I'm driving," he said with a shrug. This remark was rather amusing to her, and she started to laugh.

"Joe, have you ever thought about doing something else while you were driving?"

"Yes, I have..."

"Like what?"

"I've thought about becoming an actor, but I've never gotten the break I needed to jump-start my career...I've acted in some local stage productions and an independent film, but nothing major yet."

"If you believe in your talent, why don't you pursue it, Joe?"

"I don't know...I guess I just don't have the drive

like others who succeed…I give up too easily," Joe said, shaking his head.

"I think you could make it…I really do…just don't give up!"

"Thank you for your encouragement, but the thing is I'm not so sure whether I still have what it takes after trying for so many years…"

When the waiter came to fill the coffee, Debbie looked at her watch and panicked.

"Oh, my God…it's already after one." She got up, kissed Joe, picked up her bag, and said as she was leaving, "thanks for lunch…call me this evening."

As she rushed out of the restaurant, Joe watched her for as long as possible. He finished his coffee before returning to work.

# CHAPTER 10

MELBOURNE IS a city with an aristocratic air, with a long past and traditions. People here are serious about which school you went to and who your family is. This proud city of parklands, imposing churches, and banks of the Victorian era rarely fails to impress those who visit here. Melburnians call their city the theater capital of Australia.

In a prestigious members-only country club in Melbourne, Mr. Mulligan, Mr. McMurry, and Arnold were playing golf on a gorgeous, sunny day. Each of them pulled his golf cart along the fairway. The three of them enjoyed each other's company in addition to being important business partners in the New Age Electronics Corporation. They controlled every aspect of the company's business—from board meetings to the hiring and firing of employees. The bonds between them were so strong that nobody in the company dared to challenge them. They used this kind of golf outing to discuss everything from personal matters to business matters.

On the eighth hole, Mr. Mulligan took a couple of practice swings and teed off first while Mr. McMurry and his son looked on.

"Oh, my!…what a beautiful shot that is!" Mr. McMurry said. Arnold clapped his hands while Mr. Mulligan was beaming at his swing.

"Al, it's your turn now," Mr. Mulligan said. Mr. McMurry placed his ball on the tee.

"I hope I can match your shot," he said as he took a preparatory motion. He swung and hit the ball; it curved to the left and landed in a wooded area.

"Doggone it!… I always pull it to the left," he said disappointedly.

When they finished playing golf, they went to the country club cocktail lounge to drink and unwind. There were hardly any other customers in the lounge. They ordered some cocktails. Their talks wandered around on various subjects before landing on company affairs.

"Hasn't our company stock risen by 10% in the last two days?" said Mr. Mulligan.

"Oh, has it, Arnold?" Mr. McMurry said, turning his head to Arnold.

"Yes, it has."

"That's wonderful news…I think we should celebrate this with a toast," said Mr. Mulligan.

"I wouldn't say that, Mr. Mulligan."

"Why is that, Arnold?"

"The sudden up-swing was due to a take-over attempt by Jay Scarsone, who is one of the most feared corporate raiders in the world," said Arnold. He added, "He hasn't made a serious move yet, but for someone with this guy's reputation, even a rumor is enough to make an impact on our stock."

"But why is he targeting our company?" Mr. McMurry asked with a confused look on his face.

"He thinks our company's net worth is more than the stock value…so, like many corporate raiders, he isn't interested in running the company once he buys it. But he will chop it up into little pieces and sell them individually…This is how they make a fast profit," explained Arnold.

"I've heard that they do that…this is rather serious…" said Mr. Mulligan. Mr. McMurry was deep in thought, and his face was as stern as could be.

He turned to Mr. Mulligan and Arnold and said, "We'd better have an emergency board meeting tomorrow."

"I'll make sure all the board members are informed," said Arnold.

They finished their drinks in silence.

# CHAPTER 11

JOE RETURNED to the Residence Club around 7:00 PM. He went up to the front desk to check his mailbox slot. He didn't find any letters, but there was a note from Debbie: "Hi, Joe, come up and see me, Debbie." He smiled, put the note into his pocket, and went up to her room. He knocked on her door, and she answered shortly after. She was wearing make-up and a white evening dress. He detected the perfume she was wearing immediately.

"Hi, you just got off work?" she said with a smile, showing light pink lipstick on her lips.

"Yup."

"Come on in," she said, pulling him into the room.

"She isn't in?" He entered the room with the look of a thief.

"Sherry has a dinner date."

He looked around the meticulously arranged room; it felt and smelled like a woman's room. Joe wondered how the same rooms in the same building could be so different depending on who occupied the rooms. Joe grabbed Debbie's waist and looked at her before giving her a long kiss. Then he asked her, like an afterthought.

"Is she going out with somebody?"

"Yes…and guess with whom?" Debbie said with a playful look.

"I have no idea, and frankly, I don't care to know…I'm just happy that she found somebody," he said with a shrug.

"But take a guess, you'll be surprised." Joe thought for a moment and said, "Barry?" She nodded.

"Oh, that son of a gun!"

"She likes him."

"Good for her…he is a nice guy."

Debbie pulled away from Joe and sat down in front of the mirror stand to touch up her lipstick. Joe came up behind her and kissed her neck.

"Do you know why I left a note in your box?" she said, looking at Joe in the mirror.

"No, I don't. Debbie, does everything have to have a reason?"

When he tried to kiss her neck again, she got up and said, "Close your eyes."

"Close my eyes?"

"Yes."

He closed his eyes and said, "Is this some kind of trick you're gonna play on me?" Debbie opened the drawer, took out a beautifully wrapped box, and handed it to him.

"Now open, Happy Birthday, Joe," she said with a kiss. When he opened his eyes, he was stunned at what he heard and what was in his hand.

"What?... Today is my birthday?"

"Yes, it is."

"That's right...How did you find out?"

"A few weeks ago, I asked the manager..." Joe scratched his head and said, "Hmmm...I'll be damned..."

"Well, are you going to open the box?" He opened it and found a watch.

"Wow...What a nice gift this is! You must have spent a lot for this."

"Now look at the back of it." He turned the watch over. On it was inscribed "Love, Debbie." He removed his old watch and put the new one on.

She looked at his face carefully and asked, "Do you like it?"

"Do I like it?... Oh, Debbie, this is the best birthday gift ever...thank you..."

He looked at her. He was speechless. He wanted to say something appropriate to express how he felt but couldn't find words that would do justice.

Their long gaze inevitably led to a passionate kiss, which in turn led to lovemaking.

At that moment, a car pulled up to the curb of the Residence Club, and out came Barry and Sherry, dressed in evening party attire. They walked inside and went to the elevator. Inside the elevator, neither of them spoke. When they got off at the third floor, Sherry extended her hand for a handshake and said, "I had a good time…thank you so much for dinner."

Barry was reluctant to shake hands, but he did so after a few seconds and said, "I'll walk you to your room, Sherry, if that's all right with you…"

She forced a smile and said, "Thank you…but I'd rather say goodbye here."

Barry grinned awkwardly.

"Maybe we can do this again…soon?" said Barry, although he knew it would be highly unlikely to ever happen again.

"Sure…" and she gave him a goodnight kiss on his forehead and started to walk away from him. Barry, dejected, watched her for a moment before he headed to his room on the second floor. On the way to his room, he thought about his date with Sherry and why things didn't click as he had hoped. When he got to his room, he started to feel bad about the whole thing. He thought that it was mainly his fault that the date was a flop. He wracked his brain thinking about what he should have done and what he should not have done, and so on. He concluded that the way to forget the painful disappointment of that evening was to drink a bottle of whiskey, hit the sack, and hope he would do better if there were a date in his dream.

What Barry didn't know was the date had been doomed from the beginning. Sherry agreed to go out with him, not because she liked him, but to show Debbie that she too could have a man any time she wanted. She was intensely jealous of Debbie's happiness. So even though she was on a date with Barry, her mind was on something else. It didn't matter what Barry said or did.

When Sherry approached her room and was about to take out the key, she heard panting sounds from within. After a moment, it was clear to her that Debbie and Joe were making love. To her, this was the ultimate humiliation; she just stood there for a while, then walked away. She didn't know where to go, so she went down to the lobby, but she couldn't sit there and read something. She went to the TV room, but it was the same situation. She was far more agitated than she realized. She walked around the building but soon realized she was heading toward Barry's room.

When she was standing in front of the door, she hesitated a couple of times before finally knocking. Barry opened it with his shirt unbuttoned, showing his bare chest with a bottle of whiskey in his hand. He was most surprised to see Sherry still in her same party dress, and he was understandably speechless.

"Can I come in?" she said. Without waiting for a response from Barry, she went in and closed the door behind her. Without uttering another word, she touched his bare chest and started to caress and kiss it as she took her clothes off. Barry thought he was dreaming.

# CHAPTER 12

IN THE FINANCIAL district in Melbourne, where skyscrapers seemed to be competing to see which was the tallest and biggest, the New Age Electronics Corporation Headquarters building stood high. Inside this building, unbeknownst to the outside world, they were fighting for its very existence, trying to thwart the takeover attempt by corporate raider Jay Scarsone. The emergency board meeting was in progress, with eleven board members seated at an oval-shaped table. Mr. McMurry was in the chairman's seat. Mr. Mulligan and Arnold were seated closest to the chairman, facing each other.

"Gentlemen, the reason I have called this emergency meeting is, as you all know by now, that our company is threatened with a hostile takeover by Jay Scarsone...We all know what kind of character he is and what his true intentions are once he acquires this company…I would like to discuss with you and hopefully reach a consensus as to what would be the best way to fend him off," the chairman said, looking at his board members attentively.

There was a steely silence among the board members. It was broken by Mr. Mulligan's question, "How much stock has he acquired so far?"

"According to the news I just received a few hours ago, he has already acquired 15% of our stock, for which he has paid $300 million," said Arnold, looking at his note pad.

"Could this be his ploy to raise the stock price and then sell all of the shares for a huge profit?" said one board member.

The chairman looked at him for a moment and said, "I suppose everything is possible…but if his past behavior is any indication, he has done that only once. So, it's safe to say we really don't know at this point what his intentions are…"

The meeting progressed late into the night with no definite answers to the dilemma.

# CHAPTER 13

At the San Francisco Ballet Academy, after long hours of rigorous exercise under the strict supervision of Katerina, the instructor finally called for a break.

"All right, girls...we'll take a five-minute break!"

Debbie and Sherry grabbed a towel, wiped the sweat off their faces, and sat down side by side.

"I'll tell you, Debbie, she's a killer," said Sherry, looking at her sideways.

"You sure can say that again," Debbie chimed.

"I'm really pooped today," said Sherry.

"What time did you get home? It must have been a good date with Barry," said Debbie, and waited for Sherry to respond.

"The date was...well...it could've been better...but the nightcap was nice, very nice," said Sherry, clearly insinuating something.

"You had a nightcap?" Debbie was surprised.

"Yes, in his room…since I couldn't use mine…Why does that surprise you, Debbie?"

"No, I'm not…it's just…well…" Debbie blushed and mumbled at the thought that she and Barry might have come to the room and heard their lovemaking last night. The moment was very awkward for Debbie until the instructor clapped her hands to signal that the exercise was resuming.

"If you care to know, Barry was wonderful," Sherry said, getting up to join the other ballerinas. Her looks and words contained sarcasm. Debbie looked at her for a couple of seconds before she got up as well.

# CHAPTER 14

DEBBIE'S FATHER, Mr. Mulligan, was very fond of reading; it was one of his favorite hobbies. He loved reading so much that it was not uncommon for him to come out of his study only for meal breaks over a whole day. So, whenever he was in his study reading, other family members tried extra hard not to bother him unless it was important.

The houseman knocked on the door a couple of times and brought a phone to him.

"Excuse me, sir, a call from Mr. Scarsone. He says it's a very important matter."

"Thank you, Fred." He bowed and left.

"Yes, Mr. Scarsone, what can I do for you?"

Mr. Scarsone was in his office with his financial advisors and a couple of lawyers when he called Mr. Mulligan.

"How are you, Mr. Mulligan…I suppose you've already heard about me and my latest business endeavor?" His voice was low, deep, and full of confidence.

"Yes, I have."

"Well, Mr. Mulligan, I'll be blunt with you. I already have the approval of five board members from your company to initiate my takeover…but to have a simple majority, I need one more vote…Are you interested in coming over to my side…I can certainly reward you handsomely if you do."

Mr. Mulligan grew agitated as he listened.

"Mr. Scarsone, I don't know how much money you have or what exactly you do for a living, but…let me tell you this once and for all…Some things are not for sale, and I am one of them. Good night, Mr. Scarsone!" He hung up the phone without giving him a chance to respond. He picked up the book, but his thoughts were on the phone call. A little later, it rang again.

"Hello…Allow me to explain one more thing to you, Mr. Mulligan. I understand that your vote is not for sale, but I also understand that every man has a price. I'm willing to offer you…twenty million dollars in cash and stock options if you accept my offer."

Mr. Scarsone thought it was a good offer or at least worth a second try, but he didn't know Mr. Mulligan. He would not have accepted it even if the offer were a billion dollars. To him, it was not a matter of money but loyalty. What he valued the most was his longtime friendship with Mr. McMurry. In fact, the offer was most insulting to him, and he was visibly upset at Scarsone's insistence.

"I've already told you that my answer is no…and no means no, Mr. Scarsone." Mr. Mulligan raised his voice.

"Well, I hear you very clearly, but I don't get easily discouraged, Mr. Mulligan…you think about my offer and give me a call if you change your mind…Good night, sir."

Mr. Mulligan slammed the receiver down and got up to call the houseman.

"Fred!…Fred!…"

He suddenly grabbed his chest and collapsed on the floor as if he had been shot. When Fred came in, he rushed to Mr. Mulligan, whose face started to turn blue. Fred was in a state of panic and didn't know exactly what to do. He rushed out of the study and called upstairs to Mrs. Mulligan. When she came out of the room, she knew instantly something was wrong with Fred's tone of voice.

"Yes, Fred…what is it?"

"Come down quickly, Madame…Mr. Mulligan has collapsed in the study, and he isn't moving," he said in a trembling voice.

As she heard what Fred said, she felt her legs get weak. However, she somehow found the energy to frantically come down the stairs to study. If she had come down any faster, she would have tripped and rolled down the stairs. Once she saw her husband lying on his side, memories flashed through her mind like instant film clips: their first date, the celebration of their first baby, their silver wedding anniversary, and so on.

She knew she had to be strong at this moment; she was surprised at her calmness in trying to revive him. She attempted CPR while Fred called an ambulance.

"Hello, hello, operator…please send an ambulance to 905 Seaview Avenue."

"What seems to be the problem? The operator said in a casual tone of voice, which irritated Fred's already strained nerves.

"A man just had a big heart attack!" he yelled.

"Is he conscious?"

"No, no…He's dying…please send an ambulance quickly… please." His voice changed to a begging tone.

Mrs. Mulligan realized the magnitude of the heart attack when everything she tried had no effect. The sinking feeling in her stomach went deeper and deeper as each second ticked away. She asked Fred to bring a wet towel to place on her husband's forehead. She held her husband's hand and prayed in earnest. She was not a religious person and had never been to a church in her life, but somehow, it was the only thing left for her to do. At that moment, she wanted to believe there was an almighty God who could help her by helping her husband. Soon, a noisy siren announced the arrival of the ambulance. The ambulance workers put Mr.

Mulligan on a stretcher, carried him out to the ambulance, and rushed him to the hospital. Mrs. Mulligan rode in the back with her husband. The more she looked at her husband's pale and unconscious face, the more the tears rolled down her cheeks.

"Oh, God…please God…don't let him die…" she said, squeezing her husband's hand firmly.

When the ambulance reached the hospital emergency unit, doctors and nurses were already waiting for Mr. Mulligan. All the heart specialists tried frantically to revive him but to no avail. As the final option, they decided to take him to surgery.

# CHAPTER 15

WHILE HER FATHER was having heart surgery a thousand miles away, Debbie was having dinner with her regular partners, Joe, Sherry, and Barry, at the Residence Club.

"How's the food, Sherry?" Barry asked.

"Let's just say that I've eaten better food before."

"I know what you mean...but for the price we pay here, I'll say it's not too bad," said Barry. Sherry took a glance at Joe, who was unusually quiet.

"How was your day, Joe? You're quiet tonight."

"Oh, I'm kind of exhausted..."

"Bad day?"

"Yeah."

"You looked tired, Joe," Sherry continued while Debbie looked at her distrustfully.

"Tell me about it...I could use a hot sauna and massage," said Joe.

"I know how to give a neck massage…if you want, just let me know."

Joe liked the offer, but the minute he saw Debbie's face, he changed his mind.

"That's O.K, Sherry…thanks anyway."

"I didn't know that you knew how to give massage…when did you learn that, Sherry?" said Barry with a twinge of jealousy, realizing that she made the offer to Joe, but not to him.

"Well, Barry, let's just say…it's all part of being a ballerina. I must take care of my body, so I learned."

"Oh, that makes sense…" said Barry, nodding his head.

At that moment, a desk clerk came by the table and informed Debbie she had a long-distance phone call. She followed the clerk to a phone booth and picked up the receiver. "Hello…"

"Debbie…Oh, my baby, Debbie…You must come back home immediately…Your father's in the hospital!" Her mother's trembling voice told her how serious things were.

"What happened, Mom?"

"He's had a heart attack and is having surgery at this moment," her mother's voice was breaking as she spoke.

When Debbie heard that, she covered her mouth in shock, and tears poured down her cheeks.

"Oh, no!…oh, no!…How can that happen to him!… Is he conscious now?" Debbie said, wiping her tears.

"No, Debbie, he is not…I just don't know what to do…Can you come back right away?"

"Yes, I'll be there as soon as possible…You must be strong, Mom…O.K.?"

"I will, Debbie…I will…" she said, fighting back her tears.

As soon as she hung up the phone, she rushed up to her room by the stairs. All she wanted to do was cry, so she lunged onto her bed and wept.

She couldn't believe how this could happen to her and turn her whole world upside down. Just a few minutes ago, she thought she was the luckiest girl in the world and her family the happiest. But now, she felt just the opposite. No matter how much she cried, she realized it wouldn't change the fact that her father might have died already. She felt like a little orphan girl who would have to struggle to survive.

She had many fond memories of her father. Since she was the only child, her father showered her with love and affection. He always made her feel she was the best, prettiest, and cutest girl in the world. There wasn't anything he wouldn't do for her if she asked. His love for Debbie was so great it even made her mother jealous at times. Likewise, Debbie also loved and respected her father with all her heart. When she started to get interested in boys in her early teens, she looked for boys who had similar features and the same qualities as her father since he was, for her, the perfect male figure.

Joe felt something was wrong when Debbie didn't come back to finish her dinner. He thought for a moment that maybe she was angry at him over the conversation he had with Sherry about a "hot sauna and massage." But he soon discarded that notion since he knew she had more class than to express her anger that way. If she were truly angry, she would have expressed it differently. He knew it had something to do with the phone call she had just received.

Maybe there was some terrible news. At any rate, he decided to go to her room and find out. He knocked on the door but there was no answer. So, he knocked again, and a little later, there was the sound of bedsprings squeaking as she got up from it.

"Debbie, it's me, Joe…"

When she opened the door, he knew something was wrong. Her face said it all.

"Something wrong?" Debbie only nodded her head.

"What?"

"My dad has had a massive heart attack, and he's having surgery at this moment."

"Really?… Oh, that's terrible…" He was just as shocked as she was.

"I have to go back as soon as possible." She went over to the phone to make an airline reservation.

"Operator, can you give me the airline reservation number?"

As she waited for the operator to tell her the number, she wiped her tears repeatedly with a handkerchief. Joe stood watching helplessly. He didn't know how to help her.

It was a cold, foggy night when Joe took Debbie to the San Francisco airport. Only a few cars were on the freeway. Inside Joe's VW, they were quiet for a long time. They didn't know what to talk about.

"I wish this was just a bad dream," she said, turning her head to Joe. "Thank you, Joe…you've been a big help," she said as she touched his hand on the stick shift. He looked at her, held her hand, and smiled, "I hope everything is all right with your dad…"

After reaching the airline ticket counter at the airport and going through check-in procedures, they heard the announcement about the departing flight to Melbourne; she had to hurry. Debbie and Joe ran to the gate. When they got there, there were only a few passengers left in line.

"I'll call you as soon as I can," said Debbie.

"Don't worry about me. You just take care of your family any way you can."

"But I'm going to miss you so much!" She hugged him, and they kissed long and hard. One of the airline staff told her that she needed to get on board. However, she didn't want to let go of him.

"You'd better get going, Debbie...you're going to miss the plane." She kissed him one more time and loosened her grip. She grabbed her bags and rushed to the gate, but turned around one last time and mouthed "I-LOVE-YOU" and waved goodbye with a smile. Joe stood there and waved back. He stood there long after the plane took off into the dark sky, wondering whether he would ever see her again.

# CHAPTER 16

THE PLANE LANDED in Melbourne around 1 PM. Although the sixteen-hour flight had been long and tedious, Debbie felt good to be back. She rushed through the airport to get to the hospital as soon as possible. She got into the first one in a long line of taxis and told the driver to hurry, if possible, promising him a good tip.

It was about a 30-minute drive from the airport to the hospital, the city's finest. She asked a nurse at the information desk: "Could you please tell me where Mr.

Mulligan is?"

"Certainly," she said and checked the in-patient sheet.

"He's in room 209."

Debbie thanked the nurse and walked down the

second-floor hallway, checking the room numbers as she went by. When she finally found it, she took a deep breath before knocking. When Debbie and her mother saw each other, they were speechless. They just hugged each other and cried on each other's shoulders for a long time.

"Oh, Debbie, my baby…let me look at you…" Her mother held her face with both hands.

"I'm all right, Mom…how is daddy?" She went over to her father. She gently touched his forehead and kissed his cheek. He had a tube in his nose to help his breathing and many cords and tubes attached to his body to monitor his heart activity.

"His condition has been improving steadily, but he's not out of the woods yet," her mother said in a hushed voice lest he might hear it.

"When was he moved to this room?"

"This morning."

There was a knock on the door. A doctor and a nurse entered to check on the patient. Dr. Tully was very tall, in his early fifties, and had an imposing presence about him. His eyes were bright and sparkling clear, but at the same time, he had a look of a humorous nature. He always joked with his patients and their families. Some people took Dr. Tully's demeanor as insufficiently serious for a heart surgeon. They felt that somehow, he was not trustworthy, but when it came to actually doing heart surgery, no one was more serious than he. To him, joking around was his way of releasing the stress and tension of his job.

"Hello, how's he doing, Mrs. Mulligan?" the doctor said with a smile.

"I think he's doing OK…Oh, Dr. Tully, this is our daughter, Debbie."

"Hi, Debbie…I must say your father is a lucky man in more ways than one…Normally, the kind of heart attack that your father experienced is fatal 95% of the time, but he somehow survived it. However, I must caution you that he is not out of the woods yet…but he is steadily recovering, and that is a very good sign."

"Thank God…Oh, thank God!" Debbie said as she covered her mouth.

"Like I said, he is a very lucky man!" he said, smiling at her.

"I'm so happy that he's all right…thank you, Doctor Tully."

"I think it was your prayers that made the difference."

The nurse checked the computer monitor paper tape and jotted down the information on a log sheet. The doctor checked Mr. Mulligan's heart condition with a stethoscope.

"Everything looks normal…well, Mrs. Mulligan, Debbie, he still has some ways to go before a full recovery…so keep your fingers crossed."

"We will, Doctor…we will…" Mrs. Mulligan said.

When the doctor and the nurse left, Debbie went over to her father and whispered in his ear.

"Hi, Daddy, it's me, Debbie…you're going to be all right, Daddy…you're going to be all right…" She kissed him softly and rubbed her face against his. As her mother looked on, she saw tears well up in her daughter's eyes.

# CHAPTER 17

DEBBIE WAS EXTREMELY tired after the visit to the hospital. The fatigue of her long flight and the tension and anxiety of not knowing her father's condition all came tumbling down on her. So, when she got to her house, she could manage only a brief exchange of greetings with Fred and collapsed onto her bed immediately. She was still asleep at ten in the morning when Fred knocked on her door.

"Miss Mulligan, breakfast is ready. Can I come in?"

The knocking woke her up, and she sat upright on the bed.

"Miss Mulligan, breakfast is ready...Can I come in?" Fred repeated. She instinctively touched up her hair, trying to look presentable. "Yes, come in."

Fred brought in a breakfast tray and put it carefully in front of her.

"Oh, this is wonderful, Fred...I haven't had this for a long time."

"Mrs. Mulligan has already left for the hospital. She instructed me to give you breakfast in bed."

"Oh, that's very sweet of you, Fred. What time is it?"

He looked at his watch and said, "It's ten minutes after ten, Miss Mulligan."

"Already?... I guess I'm going to suffer jet lag for a while..."

"You'll get over it in no time, Miss Mulligan...enjoy your meal, and if you need anything, just pick up that phone, and you know what to do, right?"

"Thank you, Fred."

He bowed and left. She looked at the breakfast tray and was pleasantly surprised that everything was cooked exactly the way she liked it. She realized once again how pampered a life she had led. She looked around her room and found everything the same, as if she had never gone away. While she was enjoying her meal, the phone rang. It was from none other than Arnold. Although her heart jumped, her voice was calm.

"Hello, Arnold?... I'm fine...and you?"

He was calling her from his office on the 32$^{nd}$ floor of the company building overlooking the city and the ocean and everything there is to see.

"When did you come back?... It's so good to hear your voice, Debbie."

"Yesterday…I was going to call you, but I was in the hospital all day."

"Yes, I understand…I should've gone there to see him, but I was so busy…how is he, Debbie?" "He's improving fast. He is doing well…"

There was a pause for a couple of seconds.

"Listen, Debbie, I'm simply dying to see you…We have so much to talk about. I am up to my ears in things to do, but for you, I'm going to drop everything. Why don't we have lunch together today?"

She wanted to say tomorrow or some other day, but Arnold's voice was too forceful for her to refuse. Besides, she said to herself, what good would it do to put it off for a couple of days? She thought she might as well face it today.

"…That's a good idea…" she said hesitantly.

"Good. I'll pick you up at one."

"O.K…see you…"

She hung up the phone, put the tray aside, and looked up at the ceiling as she thought about the meeting with Arnold.

# CHAPTER 18

Arnold arrived punctually at one. He was dressed in a dark, pinstriped suit. He got out of his Jaguar, holding a bouquet, walked to the front door, and rang the doorbell. Debbie, wearing a beige dress and sunglasses, came out promptly. She gave him a hug and a kiss as she received the flowers from him.

They went to a five-star restaurant. The waiter was prompt and courteous. He served them with utmost care. The food and drinks were excellent, but her heart was in such turmoil that Debbie just couldn't enjoy them.

"Did you enjoy your stay in San Francisco?"

"Yes, I enjoyed it very much…" "What did you enjoy the most?"

"Well, the city is so gorgeous and beautiful…and I like the training I was receiving…it's not easy but I didn't expect it to be…"

"Anything else you like about the city?"

"It's such a cosmopolitan city, and I've met a lot of interesting people."

"Oh, I see…what kinds of people?" Arnold's inquisitiveness made her a little uneasy.

"Well, there are people from all over the world…I got to meet them because I stayed at a boardinghouse."

"I see…now you've got me excited about that place, Debbie…Maybe we can go there on our honeymoon?"

Debbie was taken aback when she heard the word "honeymoon." Arnold looked at her and waited for her to respond.

"…Yes, I suppose…that's not a bad idea…" It was not the enthusiastic answer that he was looking for.

"You don't seem to be thrilled at my suggestion." His voice was accusatory.

"Why, Arnold?… I said that's not a bad idea."

"I know that's what you said…but Debbie, I've known you long enough…I think you owe me an explanation… just don't play games with me."

"What are you suggesting?" She raised her voice.

He looked at her for a moment. "I've started to notice in your letters that something's not the same."

"What's not the same?.. Can you be a little more specific?"

"Well, for one thing, your letters have gotten shorter and shorter."

"Maybe I've been busy…" she said with a shrug.

"Come on, Debbie…Why don't you level with me?… If you said that you've met someone new…I would understand…"

She felt cornered. She picked up a glass of water and took a drink while thinking about how to respond to the onslaught of questions.

"Arnold, we've been friends since we were little kids, and I've always liked you…I've felt that you were the brother that I've never had…You're so talented and likable that I feel my mother likes you more than I do… but, Arnold, I've always felt that our marriage was prearranged by your parents and mine…I never really had any say in this. I want to know who I am…We need to know what we want, not what our parents want us to do, Arnold…I think it will be so much better if we wait until we're ready for each other…I really do…"

Arnold stared at Debbie after she finished her monologue.

"Well?" she said, trying to elicit a response from him.

"My dear, Debbie…you've spoken so eloquently, but you still haven't answered my question…Is there a new man in your life?"

She wanted to deny it, but she knew the time had come to tell the truth, no matter how painful it might be. She paused a few seconds to gather courage and said, "Yes…"

When he heard her faint and yet unmistakable

answer, he closed his eyes to endure the pain. When she saw this, she felt sorry for him.

"I'm sorry, Arnold…I'm truly sorry…" She wanted to comfort him, but she also knew no words could ease his pain. He put his head down for a moment, then raised it and said, "That's all right…please don't feel sorry for me…" He forced a smile and added, "He must be one hell of a guy to have swept you off your feet."

She just hung her head, not knowing how to respond.

Looking at her made him miserable about the whole thing.

"I'll take you home," he said, getting up from the table.

On the way back, they didn't talk for a long time; Arnold drove, and Debbie looked outside to avoid eye contact.

"So, tell me, Debbie…What kind of guy is he?" he said teasingly.

"I'd rather not, Arnold," she said without moving her head.

There was another moment of silence.

"Are you going to tell your mother that our marriage is off, again…indefinitely this time?"

"Yes, I'll tell her."

"It's kind of funny…your mother and mine were so sure that we were going to tie the knot this time that they even set a tentative wedding date…Maybe that jinxed it."

"I'm so sorry, Arnold…this is all my fault…"

"No, Debbie, I don't want you to feel sorry for me…I can't stand somebody feeling sorry for me…I want you to be happy, no matter what you do."

Distraught with guilt, she squeezed her head with both hands.

"You and your family have been so good to me…I just can't bear thinking that I'm going to disappoint them in any way…"

"Don't worry about them, Debbie…I'll handle my side…just promise me one thing…that you're not going to do something that you'll regret later…and if you should change your mind later on, I'm always willing to take you back."

She looked at him with a deep sense of gratitude.

"Yes, Arnold, I'll promise…thank you…" Her voice choked, and tears welled up in her eyes.

They arrived at her house at four in the afternoon. He opened the car door for her and walked her to the front door.

"When are you going back?" he said.

"I haven't decided yet…"

"I'd like to see you before you go back."

"It seems my dad is not going to be at the hospital very long…his prognosis is good…so I'm thinking in about two weeks…"

"Can I see you this weekend?" Debbie looked at him and smiled.

"Can you pick me up at six on Saturday?"

"I will," he said and kissed her on the cheek. He got into the car and drove off. She stood in the driveway and watched the car until it disappeared. As his car slowly went out of view, she felt somehow that the burden of telling Arnold about her change of heart had been lifted.

# CHAPTER 19

WHEN SHE ENTERED THE HOUSE, she almost ran into her mother, coming down the stairs in a hurry to greet Arnold. Her mother was perplexed that Arnold was not with her.

"Debbie, what happened?... Isn't he coming in for some tea?"

"No, Mom..." She was surprised at her daughter's lethargic voice.

"Why? Did you two fight?"

"No, Mom." She went upstairs to her room, and her mother followed.

"Then why did he just leave?... He was dying to see you while you were gone!"

As Debbie was changing her clothes, she said, "Mom, we're not little kids anymore. We're very capable of making our own decisions."

"Something happened between you and Arnold, didn't it?"

"No, we're still good friends…it's just…"

"It's just what?!"

She wasn't ready to tell her mother what had happened during lunch, but she knew it was too late. She looked at her mother, drew a deep breath, and said, "We've decided that we're not going to get married this fall…" and looked at her mother.

"If not this fall…then when, Debbie?"

"We've decided to postpone it indefinitely until we're ready for each other."

Mrs. Mulligan was utterly speechless. She stared at her daughter, trying to gather her thoughts. Debbie was a good daughter, but she also had a stubborn streak that her mother knew better than anyone. That characteristic Debbie had gotten from her father.

"You keep saying 'we' but I have a sneaky feeling it's 'I'." Mrs. Mulligan's voice was downright accusatory. Without responding to her mother, Debbie just left her room and went to the kitchen to get a drink. Her mother followed like a shadow. After drinking a glass of milk, Debbie said, raising her voice, "You're right, Mom…it's my idea…Are you satisfied?

"Why, Debbie…but why?"

"I know that you're very fond of him, but, Mom, please try to understand if you can…It's me who's going to get married…Do I have any say in this?"

"I just don't believe what I'm hearing from you…Of course you do, Debbie!… That's why I am asking you!"

Debbie was furious but tried not to get into a shouting match with her mother. She knew how concerned her mother was in this matter. She took a couple of deep breaths and said, "I'm also very fond of him…and I know he is a very nice man…but to me, that's not a good enough reason to marry someone. I need…someone a little more special…Do you know what I'm trying to say?"

As Mrs. Mulligan listened to her daughter, it suddenly dawned on her that she meant someone other than Arnold. She now understood what Debbie was referring to. She looked at Debbie calmly for a moment.

"Yes, I think I know what you mean, Debbie…so, you think you've found that person in San Francisco?"

"Did I say that?"

"Well, it's very obvious, isn't it?"

Debbie was silent. She couldn't deny it. Her mother interpreted the silence as agreement.

"So, what does he do?… I suppose he has a job."

"Yes, he has a job…but I'd rather not go into details just yet…I'll tell you everything in due course." Mrs. Mulligan observed her for a while.

"I just hope that you know what you're doing, Debbie. You know, your father and I have been married for about thirty years…and I can tell you this much… marriage is not romance and candle-lit dinners and diamond rings…marriage is perseverance and responsibilities and sacrifices. I've seen so many marriages fail because they weren't realistic about it…they had no idea what it takes to make marriage work…I just hope that you don't make that mistake because, Debbie, you're my only child, and I love you."

Debbie pretended to think about what her mother had said, but in truth, she thought it was irrelevant to her situation.

# CHAPTER 20

Back in San Francisco, on a Saturday afternoon, Joe was reading a newspaper in his room when the phone rang.

"Hello."

"Hi, Joe. How are you?" It was Sherry. Her voice was very lively. "Can I ask you for a little favor?" Sherry said, with the receiver between her shoulder and cheek, as she sat on her bed, manicuring her feet.

"Yeah, shoot."

"I'm trying to hang some pictures here, but I just can't do it myself…Can you help me?"

"OK…I'll be there."

"Thanks, Joe."

Although he said yes, he felt a bit uneasy going to her room since he would be alone with her. She might put him in a compromising situation that he couldn't get out of. But he soon discarded this notion as the product of an overly active imagination; she might simply need someone to help her.

After she hung up the phone, she went to the mirror stand to check her make-up and put on a little more lipstick and perfume.

When Joe knocked on her door, she opened it with a big smile. She was wearing skintight pants and a tank top that showed her slim waist and belly button. The strong odor of perfume and cosmetics made him dizzy. He wanted to finish the job and get out of the room as soon as possible. Sherry had a couple of framed ballet pictures on her bed. He looked at them and said, "Nice pictures…Where do you want to hang these?"

"Let me see, I want this picture to go above the desk and the other one on that wall."

Joe got up on a chair to drive nails into the walls and hang the pictures. While he worked on it, she looked at his body with an ulterior motive. Joe quickly finished the job.

"Well, that was easier than I thought." He stepped down from the chair.

"Thank you, Joe…you're a big help."

"Anytime, Sherry."

"I don't know how to thank you."

"Don't mention it, Sherry…I don't mean to hurry, but I need to get back to my room; I was doing something."

When he tried to leave, Sherry was blocking the door.

"Excuse me, you're blocking the door."

"Yes, I know…" she said with a mischievous look.

When he looked at her, she was gazing at him with a dreamy look in her eyes. She then purposely bent over slowly to retie her shoe, showing the sexy curvature of her lower body in skintight pants. She stood and checked the reaction in his eyes as if to say…"If you were a man, how could you resist this?"

"I don't know why you're doing this, Sherry…Can you move aside?"

"I want you to make me…"

Joe knew she had a naughty, impulsive side. He was tempted to play up to her. Looking at her finely tuned athletic body, he found it hard to suppress his desire. But he knew the consequences of this might cost him dearly. If she were to tell Debbie that she had slept with him, his relationship with Debbie would be over. He knew Sherry was quite capable of doing just that.

Although Sherry and Debbie were similar in many ways, there were many differences as well. Both were extremely attractive; both exuded the kind of femininity men liked; both shared the passion of becoming prima ballerinas. But Sherry was the jealous type; it was one of her less attractive qualities. Her jealousy made her think she wanted Joe; she did not want him because of who he was. If Debbie had not been there to make her feel jealous, she could have cared less about Joe. Jealousy is an emotional beast that can make people do some very illogical things.

"I don't know what you have in mind, but I am afraid I can't, Sherry…"

When he touched her shoulder to move her aside, she threw herself at him like metal being pulled into a magnet.

He was forced to hold her.

"Sherry!"

She tried to kiss him and succeeded, but he didn't kiss her back.

"Joe, you don't know how jealous you make me whenever you look at Debbie."

"I make you jealous?"

"Yes, enough to make me feel worthless and unwanted."

"But you have Barry, and I thought you two liked each other…"

"But I want you, Joe…Can't you understand that?"

He stood still, not knowing how to respond, while she buried her face in his chest.

"I like you, Sherry, and we're good friends…"

"Don't you want me, Joe? Don't you think I'm pretty?"

"I think you're beautiful, Sherry, and I know a lot of guys who would just love to go out with you…I just happen to be in love with Debbie, and I think it's true love for me."

She looked at him intently and asked, "You really mean it, don't you?" He nodded. Sherry realized that she couldn't seduce him no matter how hard she might try. Feeling completely dejected, she pushed him away, threw herself onto the bed, and wept.

"Get out, Joe…get out…I hate you!… I hate you!"

He left the room quietly and walked down the hallway, but he could hear her weeping for some time.

# CHAPTER 21

On Saturday evening, Arnold picked Debbie up at six as promised; they went to a fancy restaurant. Debbie wore a beautiful black evening dress for the occasion. Mrs. Mulligan was most happy that she went out with Arnold. If the two were going out to spend time together, she thought there was a chance that Debbie might come to her senses and realize how lucky she was to have Arnold.

"When are you leaving?"

"Next Saturday, five in the afternoon."

"Who's taking you?"

"My mother."

Arnold played with his wine glass a while before drinking it up.

"Did you tell your mother about that?"

"Yes, I did…"

"What was her reaction?" Debbie shrugged.

"She was disappointed...you know how fond she is of you...I've never seen her object to something so emphatically...she was disappointed, and that's an understatement."

He stared at her for a moment.

"I'm going to ask you this, whether you give me a straight answer or not..."

"What's that?" His resolute tone of voice made her anxious.

He paused for a moment.

"What is the one thing...he can do for you that I can't, Debbie?" She had to think for a second.

"I don't know how to express it, but...he makes me feel alive and happy," and her face lit up as she spoke.

"How does he do that?"

"It's not so much what he does, but just being with him..."

"Why can't I be like that to you?"

"I don't know...I wish I knew..."

"Do you think that special feeling is going to last forever?"

"I don't know, Arnold...I haven't thought about it."

"Think about it...I may not be as much fun as he is...but I can provide a lot of other things for you."

"Arnold, don't you think some things are more important than money or material things?"

"I'm not denying that…but you should also know that love does not solve all problems either."

"Yes, that's true, I'm aware of that…but I've yet to find anything more important than being in love."

He was surprised at how much she was in love with this guy in San Francisco. Arnold was extremely jealous of him, a feeling he had never experienced. If he ever met him, he would have challenged him to a duel or at least to a fistfight with the winner taking Debbie.

# CHAPTER 22

THE NEXT DAY, Sunday, Mr. Mulligan left the hospital. Dr. Tully came in for a final checkup on his patient. He asked a few questions to test his brain function.

"What is five times five?"

"Twenty-five."

"Very good, Mr. Mulligan. Then what is the name of the last book you read?" He had to think for a moment.

"Human Bondage by Somerset Maugham." When he showed that he was able to answer it, the two women clapped their hands. Dr. Tully asked a few more questions, but he had no problem answering them.

"Very good, sir." He turned around and said to Debbie and Mrs. Mulligan, "It seems Mr. Mulligan has recovered remarkably. The kind of heart attack that he experienced normally blocks the flow of blood to the brain, and thus brain damage is very common, but I see no sign of it…he is indeed a lucky man."

The two women went over to Dr. Tully and shook his hand.

"Thank you, Dr. Tully…Thank you for everything…"

"You're very welcome…take good care of him and don't let him do anything too strenuous, O.K.?"

"We will, Doctor, thank you so much." Their eyes filled with tears of joy. Dr. Tully signed the release paper, gave it to a nurse, and left.

Mr. Mulligan was left in a wheelchair pushed by a hospital worker with a nurse following closely. Debbie and her mother followed them, carrying bouquets from well-wishers. A van, which accommodated wheelchairs with an electric lift, stood waiting.

"Thank you for everything…I really don't know how to thank you," said Mrs. Mulligan to the nurse. Mrs. Mulligan and Debbie exchanged hugs with the nurse and the hospital worker.

# CHAPTER 23

LATE IN THE afternoon on Monday inside the New Age Electronics Corp. headquarters, Arnold made a few business calls and sank back into his chair. He looked out the window, where the view was magnificent, and so was the weather. His secretary, a charming red-haired woman in her mid-thirties, entered his office with a bundle of files and placed them on his desk.

"Did Jay Scarsone call?" he asked as he shuffled the files.

"Yes, he called about two hours ago and said he would let you know his final offer by tomorrow."

"Thank you, Jane."

He leafed through the files and signed all the papers that required his signature. After that, he put his leg up on the desk and looked out the window. His gaze soon stopped at a framed picture of himself and Debbie taken during a fishing trip. They looked very much like a happy couple having a great time together. His thoughts dwelled on two main issues: how to get rid of Jay Scarsone and how to bring Debbie back into his life.

He truly loved Debbie in his own way. They had known each other since childhood. Their relationship was not a hot and wild romance. But they shared similar backgrounds, hobbies, and lifestyles, and this led to a strong bond of respect and friendship that over time developed into romantic love. This is why it was a shocking revelation to Arnold that she was so much in love with another man. He hoped the infatuation was temporary, that she might later come to her senses, realize how wrong she was, and decide to come back to him. For this to happen, he had to be patient at all costs. However, whenever his thoughts reminded him that her heart belonged to someone else at this very moment, he felt a sense of deep emptiness in his heart. He felt helpless, and at times anger erupted in not knowing how to get her back. So, he made a conscious effort not to think about it but to focus instead on the pressing matter of a hostile takeover of his company.

He knew he was at a crossroads in his life in more ways than one. As far as his career was concerned, it all depended on how he handled Scarsone's hostile takeover attempt. If he were successful in fending him off, it could propel him to a leadership position in the company. If he blundered, it would be hard to convince other board members to promote him to his father's position, no matter how much his father wanted him to assume that position. The company's future was literally in his hands. His father had assigned him as the person in charge of fending off Scarsone. His father had groomed him since his college days, and now it was time to test what he was made of. Although, like most fathers, he was confident that his son was up to the task, he was secretly worried, even scared at times that he might not be able to pull it off.

Arnold certainly felt the pressure to do well. He didn't want to disappoint his dad. He respected his father enormously in many ways. His father was there whenever he needed any kind of help. Now, he felt it was his turn to reciprocate. He spent hours and hours to find a solution and arranged meetings with paid financial advisors and lawyers to advise him on this matter. He spared no cost in this endeavor.

He finally concluded that what Scarsone wanted was to buy the company and then sell off its subsidiaries for a profit since the company stock was undervalued. The sum of its many parts was worth more than the total stock price. Arnold decided to implement a "poison pill" strategy by issuing a new series of "preferred stock" that gave shareholders the right to redeem it at a premium price after the takeover. This "poison pill" strategy raised the acquisition price, much to the dismay of Scar-sone. He had no choice but to abandon his attempt at a hostile takeover since there was little or no profit at all given such a high cost of acquisition. Like a beaten dog, Jay Scarsone decided to cut his losses; he made an unceremonious exit.

# CHAPTER 24

ON WEDNESDAY EVENING, Mr. Mulligan made a phone call from his study to Mr. McMurry.

"Hello, Albert, this is Bill."

He received the phone call in the living room, where his wife was reading a book.

How's your recovery going?"

"I'm doing just fine. I no longer have to use the wheelchair, and you don't know how good that makes me feel. How's everything with the company?" he asked as he walked around the room.

"Everything is under control," Albert said confidently.

"Whatever happened to that guy?... What's his name?... You know, the guy who tried to make a hostile takeover bid...Jay Scarsone, that's who!"

"Don't worry, Bill...Arnold really did a good

number on him. So good a job that not only will he be unsuccessful with his bid, but he's going to lose some money, it seems…" and he gave a hearty laugh.

"That's wonderful news, Al. You have a capable son to follow in your footsteps."

"Well, I think you're right, Bill. I'm getting a little too old for this. I'm seriously thinking about promoting him to CEO and letting Arnold take over the company's day-to-day affairs."

"I think that's not a bad idea…this Scarsone affair proves that he's a world-class businessman."

"Then, with your blessing, I'm going to make it official on Thursday at the board meeting. Can you come?"

"Sure, Al, come hell or high water, I'll be there." They shared another hearty laugh.

# CHAPTER 25

THE BOARD MEETING was in progress as scheduled, with all of its members present and seated. When Mr. McMurry, the chairman, entered the conference room, everybody got up.

"Please be seated, gentlemen," he said as he sat down first, and everybody followed suit.

"Gentlemen, today's meeting is special because I do believe the time has come for me to step down as CEO of the company, although I will stay on as chairman of the board. I've held both positions for the last 20 years. However, now is as good a time as any since Arnold proved himself beyond a shadow of a doubt by repelling the hostile takeover bid in such a grand fashion. So, I would like to nominate my son, Arnold McMurry, as my successor to the position of company CEO. Please raise your hand if you concur with me."

Every board member raised a hand. The chairman stood up and gestured to his son to come over to his side. As Arnold went to his father's side, all the board members rose in unison and applauded. When father and son hugged each other, other members went to congratulate Arnold. He shook hands with each of them.

"Congratulations, Arnold!" said Mr. Mulligan.

"Thank you, Mr. Mulligan…without your blessing, I know it wouldn't have been possible."

"You deserve everything you're getting," he said, patting Arnold on the back.

"Thank you, sir…I'll do my best."

"I know you will, Arnold."

The proud father listened to their exchanges but decided to interrupt.

"Bill, we'll have a company party this Saturday celebrating the changing of the guard…Why don't you bring Nancy and Debbie along?"

"Of course…I'm sure they'll be most thrilled to come."

That afternoon, New Age Electronics Corporation held a press conference regarding the hostile takeover matter to calm shareholders' worries. Only major newspapers and broadcast networks were invited. A horde of photographers was on hand to take pictures when Arnold showed up with his entourage. From the podium, he made a brief statement regarding his company's present condition and the robust outlook for this year's prospective earnings, which exceeded many financial analysts' estimates.

As soon as his speech was over, the journalists were eager to ask questions.

"Is it official that you're the new CEO of this company?

"Yes."

"How will you run this company's day-to-day affairs?"

"Very carefully," he said half-jokingly; his response evoked some laughs from the press.

"Why such a sudden change of the guard? Any specific reasons?" asked a blonde financial correspondent in her twenties wearing a red dress and heavy makeup.

"Well, I'd rather not comment on that…you should ask the board members."

"What really happened to Mr. Scarsone's takeover attempt, and why did he suddenly decide to abandon it?" another journalist asked. Arnold paused for a second before answering.

"He tried, I mean really tried. He used all the tactics he knew; he even resorted to questionable tactics. Consequently, we even had to replace five board members, and we suffered some financial losses, but in the end, we beat him. To me, that's all that matters. I hope he learned a thing or two and doesn't attempt another hostile takeover soon," Arnold said confidently.

"Can you explain how you were able to do that?" the same journalist asked a follow-up question.

"You already know, but the 'Poison Pill' strategy was our last option, and it worked…Like they say, 'Sometimes you eat the bear and sometimes the bear eats you'…I appreciate all of you coming…Have a nice day."

Some of the journalists tried to ask more questions, but Arnold waved them off and went out of the conference room.

# CHAPTER 26

THAT EVENING at the Mulligan mansion, the whole family was having dinner. Fred stood by in the corner.

"I have very happy news to announce." Mr. Mulligan was beaming.

"Oh, what is that, dear?" his wife said, opening her eyes wide.

"Our soon-to-be son-in-law, Arnold, officially became the CEO of our company…the new Chief Executive

Officer!"

"Oh, really, when?" Mrs. Mulligan was thrilled.

"Today. We made it official at the board meeting."

"Oh, that's so wonderful!… I knew he'd be successful, but I didn't expect it would happen so early in his life."

Debbie's mother could not hide her joy at the news,

but Mr. Mulligan noticed Debbie was strangely quiet. Mrs. Mulligan knew the reason but acted as if she hadn't noticed it.

"Isn't that wonderful, Debbie?" her mother asked.

"Yes…that's great…" she gave a faint smile. Sensing a lack of enthusiasm in her response, Mr. Mulligan looked at her again.

"What's the matter, Debbie? Aren't you feeling well?" he said with a worried look.

"No, Dad, it's just…I had a very long day shopping, and I'm kind of exhausted…" and she gave him another faint smile.

"Why so much shopping?"

Debbie hesitated a second or two before she spoke.

"I'm going back this Saturday, and I was buying some gifts for my friends in San Francisco."

"This Saturday? That's the day we're having a party celebrating Arnold's promotion…Now, you're not going to miss that, are you?"

Mrs. Mulligan quietly observed the two.

"But I already told my school and my friends that I was coming back, Daddy…"

"I don't believe you're saying this…Arnold just got promoted as the new CEO, but you don't want to attend his party because you told some people that you're going back?!… What's going on, Debbie?" He was losing patience.

"Well, Dad…it's hard for me to explain to you,

but…" She struggled to explain her position but couldn't bear thinking how much he would be disappointed to hear that she had a new man in her life.

"What is it, Debbie? You can tell me."

Mrs. Mulligan couldn't stay quiet any longer and decided to speak on her daughter's behalf.

"I can explain to you, dear." Her husband turned his head. "You see, Debbie doesn't want to marry Arnold, and she's already told him that."

Mr. Mulligan looked perplexed; he turned to Debbie, whose face had the sad look of the Mona Lisa.

"Doesn't want to marry Arnold?… Why?"

Debbie was almost in tears as she spoke, "I know it's very hard for you to believe this, but…Dad, I met somebody I really love." He put the fork down and looked at her with a cold stare.

"Now, Debbie, I didn't send you to San Francisco to fall in love with some hippie!… I sent you there to study ballet!… Is that what you were doing the whole time?"

"I'm sorry to disappoint you, Dad…I really am…but I can't change how I feel." Her voice was cracking, but her Dad was unsympathetic. He got up abruptly and threw his napkin on the table.

"I'm not going to listen to your nonsense anymore!… Debbie, cancel the flight and make sure you attend the party…that's a lawful order!" He left the dining room and went into his study. Mrs. Mulligan went over to her daughter and consoled her.

# CHAPTER 27

THAT NIGHT, Debbie's heart was in turmoil. She had trouble sleeping. She thought about many things; running away to San Francisco to marry Joe, never coming back to her family, asking Arnold to tell her parents that they had decided not to marry and that this was in the best interest of both. However, all of this was wishful thinking. She would not ask Arnold such a favor; her pride wouldn't allow it. Even if he did, there was no guarantee that her parents would be persuaded.

She finally fell asleep at dawn. She woke up a few hours later. During her brief sleep, she had a dream that she and Joe were married and had two children, a son named Kevin and a daughter named Sarah. Kevin took after herself and Sarah, Joe. They were very happy and did many things together. Joe was very good with the children, and they adored him. Debbie was so happy and thought in her dream that nothing would take this happy family away from her.

When she awoke and realized that it was a dream, she was deeply disappointed. No matter how hard she tried to hold on to it, the dream was fading fast from her memory. Yet the dream was so real she could still remember the faces of the children; had she seen them on the street, she would have recognized them easily. But now, as she sat up in her bed, she felt robbed of her happiness. The more she thought about the dream, the worse she felt.

So, she got out of bed and took a shower. When she finished dressing, she went to the window and raised the blinds. The bright sunlight flooding her room made her eyes squint. She opened the door to the verandah and went out. From the second story, she could see the beautifully manicured lawn and many kinds of flowers. The perfect blend of fresh, chilled air and the warm sunlight touching her face made her feel very good.

She was basking in the sunlight with her eyes closed when she heard knocking sounds. When she went inside, she heard Fred's voice.

"Miss Mulligan, may I come in?"

She opened the door. He entered carefully as if trying not to disturb anything.

He surveyed her face. Having witnessed what

happened last night at the dinner table, he was extra careful not to upset her in any way.

"You haven't had anything to eat today. Can I bring you something?"

"No, Fred…I don't want to eat anything now."

"Then, just some tea and cookies, maybe?"

She could not help but smile when she looked at his face, full of innocence, seriousness, and concern.

"Thank you, Fred…I'd love that." He smiled.

After Fred left, she suddenly felt a strong urge to hear Joe's voice. It had been a while since she heard it. She picked up the phone and dialed. A young male voice answered the phone.

"This is the Residence Club. How can I help you?"

"Can you ring Joe Sanders, room 205?"

"Sure, just a moment." The desk clerk pushed the red button number 205 on the switchboard. Joe was sleeping; it was three in the morning. After the fourth ring, he picked up the phone, feeling ticked off that someone had roused him from sleep.

"Hello." His voice was that of a drunken sailor.

"Hi, Joe…this is Debbie…how are you?"

Although the voice was raspy, she recognized that it was his.

"Hi, Debbie…what happened?… I thought maybe you forgot all about me," he said as he scratched his head and yawned.

"No, Joe, I'll never forget you…you can count on that."

"So, how's your father?"

"He's already out of the hospital and doing very well."

"So, are you coming back soon?"

"No, I'm afraid I have to stay here a little longer… something came up unexpectedly."

"Oh, that's too bad. I've been counting the days…"

"I'm so sorry, Joe. Do you miss me?"

"Yeah, I think so."

"You think so?!" She wasn't pleased with his answer.

"I mean, I do…I miss you a lot."

"I'm dying to see you, Joe."

"Then, why can't you come back soon?"

"I just can't…please try to understand…"

"O.K…"

"Just remember that I miss you terribly, and I think about you all the time."

"I miss you too, Debbie."

"Bye, Joe, love you!" She kissed the receiver.

"Bye, Debbie." He did the same. After hanging up the phone, he sat and wondered whether he had gotten a phone call from Debbie or if it had been a dream. He slid down on the bed, covered his face with the sheet, and went back to sleep.

When Fred walked into Debbie's room with a tray of

tea and cookies and sat it down on the portable table next to her, she wasn't even aware of Fred's presence. She was lost in thought of the conversation she had just had with Joe. Fred looked at Debbie, thinking that she had the look of a little girl who had just lost her puppy dog. He quietly exited without saying anything, wondering why Debbie had that look.

# CHAPTER 28

O<small>N</small> S<small>ATURDAY</small> <small>EVENING</small>, many fancy cars and limousines were arriving at the New Age Electronics Corporation building. Two doormen and four valets were working frenetically to accommodate the arrivals. People from the local media also showed up to report the event. Mr. and Mrs. Mulligan arrived in a black Mercedes. Debbie was wearing a beige evening dress that revealed the shapely contours of her body.

A doorman greeted them. Once they entered the building, the security personnel checked the invitation card and clipped nametags on their clothes. They were guided to an elevator. The elevator girl smiled and greeted them cheerfully as she pushed the button for the 25<sup>th</sup> floor, where the party was taking place. They could tell by the sound of salsa music when they arrived on the floor that the party was in full swing. A comedian had been hired to make the party guests feel loose and jovial. An usher led the Mulligans to the table where the McMurrys were sitting. Mr. McMurry and Arnold got up to greet them.

"You're fifteen minutes late…this is the first time that you've been late for anything, Bill." Mr. McMurry and Mr.

Mulligan laughed as they shook hands.

"Oh, I couldn't help it. The traffic was terrible."

When Mr. McMurry saw Debbie, he opened his arms for a hug.

"Well, hello, Debbie, I haven't seen you for ages, it seems. You look so beautiful and different now!" He took a good look at her, kissed both her cheeks, and hugged her.

"Hello, Mr. McMurry…Mrs. McMurry…hello,

Arnold…" Debbie said courteously as she bowed her head to each one. Arnold shook her hand and studied her face, thinking something must have happened since she was supposed to return to San Francisco that day.

"I'm so glad you could come, Debbie," said Arnold.

Aware that others were watching her reaction, she forced a smile.

"Congratulations, Arnold."

"Thank you, Debbie…"

The two concerned mothers paid close attention to

their exchanges and felt somewhat relieved at what they had seen.

"Nancy, you must be so proud of Arnold…What a nice and capable young man he has grown to be."

"Yes, he has…I didn't think he would succeed his father so soon…but then what do I know about business?" The two shared a giggle and turned their faces to Arnold and Debbie, who were talking about something.

"What a lovely couple they make…"

"Yes, indeed…they look so perfect for each other…" said Mrs. Mulligan with a faint sigh.

The master of ceremonies was Jimmy Hackett, a short and stocky man in his mid-thirties. He went up to the stage and signaled the band to stop playing.

"Ladies and gentlemen, it is my great honor and privilege to introduce to you the man in whose honor we're having this great party. He is one of the most generous and nicest men that I've had the pleasure to know personally, and he is now the new CEO of this great company…Ladies and gentlemen, I give you the one and only Mr. Arnold McMurry!"

Arnold got up and went to the stage. He was given a standing ovation that lasted a good three minutes. Debbie was overwhelmed by the electricity and excitement in the air. She looked at him with a sense of awe and admiration for the first time and joined in the standing ovation. Arnold motioned them to sit down, but occasional whistles and yelling continued. He calmed the crowd down and paused for a moment before he spoke.

"I intended to make a long speech, but the long and heartwarming ovation that I received from you said it all…so I will make my speech very brief."

There was a big laugh from the crowd and more applause.

"I would like to thank you for coming. Today I want you to enjoy the party and celebrate the changing of the guard at our company…The success that we have enjoyed year after year would not have been possible without your dedication and hard work…As the new CEO of this company, I want your continued cooperation and dedication to meet the challenge of the next decade and beyond…Once again, I would like to extend my thanks to all of you…Thank you from the bottom of my heart."

The audience erupted with applause once more. Arnold returned to his table. The music resumed, and many couples went to the floor and danced.

"That was a nice speech, Arnold," Mr. Mulligan said as he patted Arnold's back.

"Thank you, Mr. Mulligan." He looked around the table to thank them for their support. When his eyes met Debbie's, she smiled broadly. This time, it was genuine, not forced.

"Debbie, do you care to dance?" He stood up, extending his hand; she gladly accepted.

The music was for a slow dance. Arnold held her closely and could feel her breathing in a slightly excited state. When he turned his head to look at her, she was more beautiful than ever. He thought it might be due to the lighting, her evening dress, or her hairstyle, but there was no denying that she was gorgeous. For a few moments, they simply stared at each other.

"Why didn't you go?" said Arnold.

"Did you want me to?"

"No...but you said you would."

"Well, let's just say that I couldn't...My dad ordered me to come..."

"So, do you regret coming?"

"To tell you the truth...not as much as I thought I would." She smiled mischievously.

From the table, the two proud parents were thrilled to see them dance together and couldn't hide their joy.

"Well, Debbie, my dear...the fact that you came is all that matters, and that's good enough for me," and he kissed her rather forcefully. When Mr. Mulligan saw them kiss, he went up to the stage and grabbed the microphone.

"Ladies and gentlemen, allow me to make a special announcement...I am most proud to say that my dearest daughter, Debbie, and Arnold, who are dancing together at this very moment, are getting married this month, and all of you are cordially invited."

The crowd exploded with applause and whistles as

balloons and confetti were released and champagne corks were popped. The music resumed, matching the upbeat mood. Arnold looked at Debbie, and he kissed her once more, long and hard. Amid all the celebration, Debbie really didn't know whether to laugh or cry.

# CHAPTER 29

In the downtown area of San Francisco, Joe's cab pulled up to the curb. He got out of the cab, holding a paper. He looked at the building address and compared it with the one he had written on the paper. This was the correct address for auditions for the leading male role in an independent movie called "Car Salesman."

Joe had found out about the audition while he was browsing through a local newspaper. The ad took up a whole page. Joe read with great interest the article about the movie they intended to make.

*"This is the story of a car salesman, Jerry Alioti, one of the top salesmen in town. However, one streak of bad luck after another has led to a slump in his sales. The greedy owner of the dealership, Ed Balanchi, is*

*unsympathetic to Jerry's plight and has threatened to fire him if his sales don't improve soon. This kind of treatment from his boss is unacceptable to Jerry since Ed personally lured him five years ago to come to his dealership from another where Jerry was a top-notch salesman. The animosity that develops between them eventually results in Jerry's firing. He goes through some difficult times trying to survive.*

*His fortune drastically changes when he meets and falls in love with a wealthy widow, Margie Smith. Margie proposes that Jerry take over a car dealership; she is willing to finance the deal. Jerry reluctantly accepts her offer but then runs a profitable dealership once he takes over. Unlike Ed Balanchi, his business motto is trust. He trains every salesperson not to violate the trust of customers.*

*On the other hand, Ed's auto dealership goes under when the greedy owner hires teenage hooligans to steal goods from department stores. His arrest is top news on local TV and in local newspapers. As Jerry watches Ed go to jail for his crime, he doesn't feel the sweet revenge that he thought he would. He feels, instead, to his amazement, a sense of sadness. He finally comes to terms with himself that the best revenge is not to be found in other people's misfortune, but simply in living well."*

. . .

Joe liked the story immediately and wanted to audition for the Jerry Alioti part; he believed he could play that role well.

When he got to the second floor, there were many men already waiting to audition for the part. He wrote down his name, address, and phone number and got a waiting number. He looked around at the men. Some were sitting, some were standing, and others were reading. They all looked smarter and better-looking than him. After some waiting, his number was called sooner than he expected. His heart jumped.

When he was guided to the audition room, he saw a bearded man with a big potbelly sitting in one corner. On the other side of the room, there were two men and a woman, all in their mid-thirties, sitting behind a desk. In front of each of them were a notepad, a pen, and the script. They introduced the bearded man as Tom and told him that he was going to read Ed Balanchi's part. Joe shook hands with him. They asked Joe a few questions and joked around a little to loosen him up. There was a script on a small portable table in the center of the room. Joe picked up the script and nervously turned the pages.

"Joe, you're going to read Jerry's part from pages five to six," said the woman in the middle. Although he was nervous, he got through it nicely.

"Have you ever acted before in a commercial production?" the man on the right with a receding hairline asked.

"Yes, I have."

"Where?"

"At a local theater, playing the young protagonist in Chekov's 'Marriage Proposal'. I was also cast in an independent movie called 'Only in America.'"

"Oh yeah, I saw that movie. Was that you who played the young boxer who got screwed by his promoter?"

"Yes."

"I thought you did well portraying the hapless boxer."

The man looked impressed with Joe. It made Joe feel good that the man had seen the only movie that he had played in. He thought that maybe this was the lucky break that he had long hoped for.

"Didn't the movie make some money? I know it got some good reviews," the man with the receding hairline asked again after jotting down a few comments on his notepad.

"Yes, I think it did."

"How come you didn't get other offers after that movie?" the man on the left asked.

"I don't know why...no luck, I guess," said Joe with a shrug.

After questioning him, they talked among themselves in a hushed voice. Joe tried to figure out what they were saying by their faces and gestures.

"Do you have an agent?" the woman asked.

"No, not at the moment."

They huddled together and talked again. It was only a minute, but it seemed a long time to Joe.

"When can you start?" the man on the right asked.

"When?… Oh, I can start any time."

"Joe, come back here next Friday at two."

"Does that mean I got the part?"

"Yes," the woman said tersely.

Joe couldn't believe he had beaten out a couple hundred competitors to get the part. He ran to the desk, shook hands with each one of them, and said, "Thank you very much."

He felt so good when he came out of the building that he jumped up and down and let out a scream of joy. Some pedestrians, however, thought he was either drunk or crazy.

## CHAPTER 30

He got into his cab and drove away. A few businessmen tried to flag him down, but he didn't want any more fares for that day, and he waved them away. He was too happy to work; he thought that he would just go home and celebrate with his friends with a couple of bottles of champagne, then call Debbie and tell her how he got the part. His mind was racing with many happy thoughts as he headed to turn in his cab. He was almost at Yellow Cab Headquarters; all he had to do was make one more right turn to get there. When he made the turn, he saw a black woman waving at his cab, crying. He decided to stop; maybe she needed help. When he stopped and got a closer look at her, he saw that she was a very attractive woman in her early twenties.

"Can I help you?" he asked, but she just kept crying.

When he repeated the question, she started to speak.

"Will you please take me to Visitation Valley?"

"I wish I could, but that's a long way from here, and I'm about to turn my cab in…I'm sorry."

"Sir, will you please?… I beg you…my son has been kidnapped, and if I don't go back soon, he might die…" She started to cry and made pathetic moaning sounds again. Joe really felt her pain.

"By whom?"

"By my ex-boyfriend…he's very violent…"

"But why is he going to kill your son?"

"He said if I don't bring $500 by six o'clock, he would kill my son…He's a pimp and a drug addict…He doesn't care anything…"

The woman's pathetic weeping was too much for Joe to ignore; he decided to comply with her request after thinking it over.

"Get in."

Joe picked up the cab radio receiver and talked to the dispatcher.

"Yellow, this is 1270. I have an emergency, over."

"Yes, 1270, what is it? Come in."

"Will you please send the police to 255 Ramona Street in Visitation Valley…I think we have a possible kidnapping and an extortion suspect, over."

"I read you, 1270…I'll do that right away."

"Also, please note that I'll be one to two hours late turning my cab in."

"I read you, 1270…Have a safe trip, Roger."

On the way to Visitation Valley, the woman thanked him profusely and told him a lot about her ex-boyfriend, Leroy. They had gone to the same high school and were going to get married, but his volcanic temper and drug use were a constant problem. When she decided to break up, he threatened to kill her, so she went away to Tampa, Florida, where her aunt lived. She helped her aunt run a dry-cleaning business. She got married to a man who had worked at the cleaners for ten years. She gave birth to a son, Jamie, and they had a happy family for the first two years. But the marriage broke off when she found out her husband was suffering from mental illness and was having severe hallucinations with ever-increasing frequency.

When she returned to see her family, Leroy had become a pimp with many women working for him. When he found out that she had returned, Leroy began to stalk her. Near her mother's house, he kidnapped her and Jamie as they were on their way to a corner store. He took her to his apartment; raped her and told her he would spare her life if she would go to work for him. When she refused, he beat her and gave her an ultimatum: if she didn't bring him $500 by tomorrow, he would kill her son. Although she was pretty and attractive, she had no idea how to sell her body to make money.

When the cab finally arrived at the destination, the woman ran to the apartment. Joe notified the dispatcher of his location, then got out and followed the woman. The pimp looked through the blinds when the taxi arrived. He cursed and banged his fist on a wall in disgust when he saw she was coming up with the taxi driver. She tried to open the door; it was locked. She banged on the door.

"Jamie, are you there?…Jamie, are you there?…

Answer me!"

Soon, there was a voice from within.

"Jamie is right here with me!"

"Open up, Leroy!… Open up!" She banged on the door again.

"Shut up, bitch!… You didn't keep your promise… Why did you bring a cabbie with you, huh?!" His voice was sharp and piercing. Joe tried to reason with him.

"Hey, Leroy, I don't know what the situation is here, but just let the kid go."

"Shut up, cabbie…You better get your ass outta here if you don't wanna die!"

The shouting and the door banging frightened the little boy; he began to cry. When the woman heard her little boy cry, she seemed more agitated.

"Leroy, is it the money you want?" Joe emptied his pocket and counted the money. "Hey, I got 87 bucks here…I'll give you this if you just let the kid go," he pleaded.

"Fuck you, cabbie, fuck you!… Say one more word, and I'll blow this kid's brains out," Leroy screamed. The boy started to cry louder. The mother banged her head against the door in sheer desperation.

"Leroy, you no-good son of a bitch!" Her voice reached a new high. "You better kill me, you no-good son of a bitch!" She screamed and threw her body at the door to tear it down. Joe was surprised at her strength. He tried to stop her. As the door started to crack and began to give way, the pimp fired a couple of shots through the door. Joe was standing in the wrong spot when it happened. One bullet went into his chest, another one into his neck. He grabbed his neck and went down hard. The lady went berserk when she saw blood all over Joe's face. The blood was spewing out of his neck.

Amid all this commotion and chaos, a police car arrived, its siren blaring.

One police officer saw Leroy running away and took off after him. The other cop, seeing Joe lying in a pool of blood, called an ambulance.

The police soon captured Leroy, handcuffed him, and put him in the back seat of the police car. An ambulance and a second police car arrived soon after.

The paramedics wrapped Joe's neck with gauze and tape to stop the bleeding, put him on a stretcher, and took him to the ambulance. The mother and son got into the second police car and left the scene. Suddenly, the crime scene was eerily quiet, as if nothing had happened.

# CHAPTER 31

AT THE HOSPITAL EMERGENCY UNIT, two doctors and two nurses worked frantically on Joe.

"Hand me a scissors," said the skinny, bearded doctor. The nurse handed it to him. After cutting the wrapped gauze and examining the wounds more closely, the skinny doctor looked at his colleague and shook his head.

"Boy, this is nasty! I don't know whether he's gonna make it."

"What happened to him?" asked the other doctor, who was heavyset and wearing a mustache.

"He's a cabbie who was trying to help a customer. He got shot by her jealous boyfriend," said a nurse as if she knew exactly what had happened.

"It must be very dangerous to drive a cab in this

city…We get this kind of case just about twice a month," said the bearded doctor.

Joe lay on the operating table, barely conscious. Everything was fuzzy like a dream. When the bullets went into his neck and chest, he felt like he had fallen into a deep, bottomless hole. No matter how much he waited to hit bottom, he just kept going down and down. Before he lost consciousness, his whole life flashed in front of him as though someone had secretly taped it and was now showing it to him. It was no more than a couple of seconds, but all the important events were there: his first baby walk, his first day in school, the bicycle his mom bought for his 7th birthday, his high school prom night, meeting Debbie, and so on.

# CHAPTER 32

AFTER DINNER, Mr. Mulligan retired to his study and was enjoying some quiet time alone reading the newspaper and drinking tea when his daughter knocked and entered the room.

"Daddy, can I talk with you?" He noticed his daughter's tone of voice was not the most cordial.

"Sure, Debbie," he folded the paper, put it on the table, and looked at her. Debbie stood quietly for a moment, whether collecting her thoughts or mustering courage; it wasn't clear to Mr. Mulligan.

"Daddy, you know that I love you more than anything in the world, but…I just can't forgive you for what you did at the party…You knew very well I wasn't ready for that yet."

He removed his reading glasses and took a sip of tea before he spoke.

"Listen to me, Debbie…ever since you were born, all my hopes and dreams have been with you…I was so proud when you won the national ballet competition… You just can't imagine how happy I was…I was determined to give you everything that a father could give to his daughter…You're my treasure, Debbie! I'm not going to give you away to some…nobody!"

"Yes, I know how much you love me…Do you think I don't know that? You've been the best father that anyone could have…I'm not questioning that…but this is my marriage, Dad!… It's a once-in-a-lifetime thing and the most important event in a woman's life…I think I'm old enough to decide for myself." She started to cry. "I'm not your little girl anymore, Dad!"

Mr. Mulligan looked at her for a few seconds and went over to her to comfort her. He gave her a tissue to wipe her tears.

"I've always done what's best for you…Have I done anything that wasn't good for you?" he pleaded, trying to hold her, but she pulled away from him.

"You should've at least respected my opinion and listened to me, Daddy!"

"But what is there to listen to, Debbie?… So you want to marry some guy that you met in San Francisco instead of Arnold, who has a good upbringing and a bright future?… That's total nonsense!"

"I'm not saying that Arnold isn't a good choice for

me…I like him very much…but you don't even know who I met in San Francisco…If I marry a man, I'm the one who has to live with him, not you, Daddy!"

"You really want to marry that guy?… Is that it?" His voice showed anger.

"You'll do that over my dead body!" He went to his armchair and sat down but soon got up again and came back to her. "Come on, be realistic…there is no better suitor for you than Arnold…Why are you trying to chase the rainbow rather than simply accept all the blessings you have right here!… I don't understand…I just don't understand…"

She stood there looking very dejected, knowing she couldn't change his mind no matter what she said or did. Realizing she had no other option but to accept her parents' wishes, she began to cry. She clenched her jaws with the determination of a person who was about to make a thousand-foot jump into the water.

"O.K, I'll marry Arnold…but don't ever expect me to forgive you for what you did at the party, Daddy!" and she stormed out of the room.

From the living room, her mother saw Debbie storm out of the study and run up the stairs to her room. She knew exactly what had transpired between her husband and her daughter. As a woman, she understood what Debbie was going through; she also knew Debbie was inconsolable.

The moment Debbie entered her room, she threw herself onto the bed and cried mournfully for a long time.

# CHAPTER 33

ON THE EVENING before the wedding day, Debbie stood in front of a full-length mirror. She and her mother were putting the final touches on the wedding dress. She looked much like Cinderella in her white wedding dress: a small waist accentuated by long legs and a small bust.

"You look so beautiful, Debbie," Mrs. Mulligan said as they both looked at her in the mirror.

"Don't you think the front neckline's a little low?"

"No, I don't think so…It looks very charming."

Even Mrs. Mulligan was surprised at how well the wedding dress looked on her daughter.

"How many people are coming?" Debbie asked as she turned sideways to look at her profile.

"I think at least 600…but don't you worry a thing, Debbie, you'll dazzle them with your beauty!"

"What time is it, Mom?"

"Oh, dear, it's already eleven thirty…You'll need a good night's sleep." She helped her get out of the wedding dress and hung it neatly in the closet. She hugged her daughter, kissed her good night, promised to wake her up early, and left the room.

Debbie removed her makeup, washed her face, brushed her teeth, and changed into her night dress. She went to bed and turned the light off but couldn't fall asleep. After tossing and turning for a while, she got up and turned the light back on. She sat staring at her face in the mirror for a long time.

She opened the bottom drawer and took out a picture of herself and Joe at Twin Peaks. She looked at it for a while before kissing it.

What was bothering her was not the pleasant jitter of tomorrow's wedding but a deep and hollow sadness at her inability to tell Joe about it. It would be too painful to tell him the news, but she felt it was her obligation to call and tell him, no matter how unacceptable it might be to him.

She knew this would be one of the hardest things she had ever had to do in her life. She picked up the receiver and dialed the number.

"Hello, can I speak to Joe in room 205?"

"Are you calling Joe?… Don't you know what happened to him?"

Debbie's heart sank.

"No, I sure don't…Is there a problem?"

"Well, Miss, I'm afraid so...He has been hospitalized and is in the intensive care unit in San Francisco General Hospital."

"Oh, my God!... When did that happen?"

"I don't know."

"Can you give me General Hospital's number?" She jotted it down and thanked him. She immediately dialed again.

"Hello, General Hospital?... Is Joe Sanders in intensive care?"

"Let me connect you," an operator responded. A moment later, a nurse came out, "ICU, can I help you?"

"Yes, is Joe Sanders in the unit?"

The nurse paused to look at her chart.

"Yes, he is."

"Can I talk to the doctor in charge?"

"Just a moment, please." The waiting seemed like an eternity. Finally, a young male voice at the other end said,

"Hi, this is Doctor Rosen..."

"Yes, I'm inquiring about Joe Sanders' condition."

"May I ask who's calling?"

For a moment, she didn't know how to answer.

"My name is Debbie...I'm his girlfriend..."

"O.K, Debbie...I'm sorry to tell you but his condition is serious...He has a bullet wound in the neck and one in the chest...We did everything we could, but his condition remains extremely critical…You might want to see him soon because we could lose him any time."

Tears streamed down her face as she listened.

"Thank you, Doctor…"

"Bye, Debbie…I'm sorry."

She hung up the phone, buried her face in her pillow, and cried for a long time. Then he stood up abruptly and wiped away her tears. It only took her minutes to decide. Although an elaborate wedding fit for celebrities was planned for tomorrow, with 600 guests invited, it seemed quite unimportant to her now. She had to go and see Joe. Nothing could prevent her from going, no matter what the consequences.

She changed hastily into her casual clothes and packed a small bag with her things. She looked at the mirror, put on some lipstick, then used the lipstick to write on the mirror, "I am truly sorry, but I must go. Forgive me, Debbie."

She carefully opened her door and walked down the stairs like a thief. She wanted to leave without meeting anyone. However, no noise ever eluded Fred's ears; he had a hearing sense comparable to that of a dog. When Debbie was about to open the front door, he suddenly came out of his room, shocked to see her leaving in such a stealthy manner.

"Miss Mulligan, where are you going at this ungodly hour?" he asked in a hushed voice.

"Shhhh…I can't explain it to you just now, Fred…I

want you to tell them tomorrow that I had an emergency, and I had to go…tell them I'll explain everything when I come back…Will you please do that for me?" she pleaded, kissing him on the cheek.

"But Miss Mulligan, you can't leave now…Your wedding is tomorrow…You can't do this!… You can't do this!"

Despite Fred's strong protest—just short of grabbing her to prevent her from leaving- she ran out and got into the car. He followed her to the car, trying to reason with her, but to no avail. She drove away from the house, leaving Fred standing alone in the chilly night. As he watched the car disappear, he shook his head in dismay. He returned to his room, dropping his head. He lay down on his bed, closed his eyes, and prayed that he would never wake up to see another sunrise. He could not bear to see Mr. and Mrs. Mulligan's disappointed and agonizing faces when they found out what Debbie had done. He could not even fathom what unimaginable heartaches this would bring to the household in which he had been a caretaker for the last fifteen years.

The more he thought about it, the more physically ill he became.

# CHAPTER 34

It was a foggy morning when Debbie arrived at San Francisco General Hospital. San Francisco General Hospital was a huge complex encompassing two whole blocks. A taxi dropped her off in front of the main entrance. Despite the maze of directional arrows, she managed to find her way to the ICU unit. Along the way, she saw many patients on stretchers or in wheelchairs being pushed by hospital workers and nurses.

On the ICU door was a sign saying only authorized personnel were allowed to enter. Debbie looked around and saw a nurse and a security guard in a glass booth. She approached the nurse.

"Excuse me, I came to see Joe Sanders…"

"Is he an ICU patient?" the nurse, her face a mass of freckles, asked as she checked the patient logbook.

"Yes."

"I see it here…May I ask about your relationship with him?"

"My name is Debbie Mulligan…I'm his girlfriend… I've already spoken with Dr. Rosen."

The nurse nodded her head and motioned for her to go in; she pushed the green button, and the double doors parted to let Debbie in. A nurse guided her to Joe's bed. Debbie was shocked at the large number of critically injured and ill people with all types of machines hooked to their bodies. It was depressing, yet at the same time, the place had an air of serene calmness—the serenity of death.

The nurse opened the privacy curtain wrapped around Joe's bed. The moment she saw him with his neck and chest heavily taped and a tube to his nose to help him breathe, tears began streaming down her face.

Joe's eyes were closed. His face seemed strangely peaceful. She approached him cautiously, touched his face, and kissed him on the forehead.

"Hi, Joe…it's me, Debbie…" she whispered in his ear. He slowly opened his eyes. At first, he didn't seem to recognize her. Then suddenly he said, "Hi, Debbie…" His voice was barely audible. Debbie was glad that he was able to recognize her. She pulled up a chair close to the bed, squeezed his hand, and kissed it again and again, rubbing it against her face. His lips made a faint smile. They looked at each other for some time without a word being spoken.

The silence was broken when Dr. Rosen showed up with a nurse for a periodical checkup.

"Hello. You must be Debbie. I'm Dr. Rosen."

Debbie got up, hastily wiped her tears, and shook hands.

"How is he, Doctor?"

He motioned for her to come outside of the curtain.

"His condition is still very shaky…You shouldn't make him talk much."

"O.K…"

"I'm sorry I can't give you any comforting news…If you have any questions, please feel free to page me after the visit."

The nurse did a routine check of his temperature and pulse rate, jotted them down on a chart, and left with the doctor.

When Debbie went inside, his eyes were closed again. He looked somehow different from a little while ago. She sat close to him and caressed his face. He opened his eyes, but he looked more tired this time.

"Joe…I missed you so much…You don't know how much I missed you…"

"Me too…"

"Do you still remember our first date?… How you showed me around the city and we went up to Twin Peaks…You remember, don't you? Oh, it seemed like only yesterday…What a wonderful, stimulating chat we had in Berkeley…Oh, how fresh and pure those moments were…" Joe's eyes welled up with tears as he listened. He said, "I remember…" with a faint smile.

She squeezed his hand and kissed it and said, "Joe, if I could relive those moments with you, I would trade anything for it…I mean anything…"

Joe smiled at Debbie. He tried desperately to say something. His lips were moving, but no sound could be heard.

"What is it, Joe?" Debbie put her ear close to his mouth and waited.

"Thank you, Debbie…Thank you for the memory… thank you for the beautiful memory…" His eyes closed as he took his last breath.

The tears that had welled up rolled down his face.

Debbie hugged him and cried as she kissed his face.

# CHAPTER 35

When Debbie walked out of the hospital, she knew what she wanted to do. She wanted to go to Twin Peaks and relive the moment of her first date with Joe.

There was a cab waiting at the taxi stand; she got in.

"Twin Peaks, please."

"The sightseeing area, Miss?"

"Yes."

As she made her way to Twin Peaks, everybody was waiting at a wedding hall in Melbourne for the bride to show up. When Debbie's parents heard that she was gone, it was too late to cancel the wedding and notify the guests. Arnold stood alone at the altar in front of the pastor, waiting for Debbie to show up. The six hundred agitated guests were told later that the wedding had been called off.

When she arrived at Twin Peaks, the weather was

clear, the views magnificent. She stood alone and looked at the city and the bridges as she tried to relive the moment. Then she thought she heard someone call out her name. She turned her head, and for fleeting seconds, she saw Joe in his Air Force bomber jacket, beckoning her to come to see something as he had done on their first date. She waved back, but Joe's image vanished just as quickly. It was an illusion like in so many aspects of our lives.

She stood for a long time, reflecting on all she and Joe had done together from their first meeting until his death.

When everything is said and done, all we have are memories, beautiful memories...

The End

## ABOUT THE AUTHOR

Kenny Lee has been teaching Global Affairs at West Valley College in San Jose since 2017, and before that, he also taught a language and culture at the Defense Language Institute in Presidio of Monterey until he retired in 2013.

He began writing in 1994 after a financial crisis of losing a house due to a bad investment. To alleviate mental anguish and depression, he began writing.

His second screenplay was Taxi Driver & Ballerina, which seemed to garner favorable reactions from people who read it. One of his close friends suggested that he turn the popular screenplay into a novel. That's how this book came about.

In his free time, he likes to travel around the world and see how people live their lives.

### I'd Love To Here From You!

Thank you so much for reading this book; it means the world to me. If you found this book enjoyable, would you take a moment to leave a review?

Your feedback not only helps others but also keeps me motivated to create more valuable content for you.

### Here's how you can leave a review:

1. Scan the QR code on this page to go directly to the review page on Amazon.

2. Or visit your Amazon Orders page, find this book, and click "Write a Product Review."

### Your kind words make a big difference.

### Thank you for your support!

*SCAN ME*

Made in the USA
Monee, IL
04 March 2025

12988788R10100